Two Blocks Down

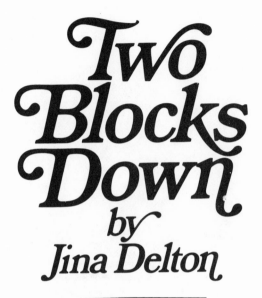

Two Blocks Down

by
Jina Delton

HARPER & ROW, PUBLISHERS

NEW YORK

Cambridge
Hagerstown
Philadelphia
San Francisco

1817

London
Mexico City
São Paulo
Sydney

Library of Congress Cataloging in Publication Data
Delton, Jina.
    Two blocks down.

    SUMMARY: A high school girl is torn between
her new friends and her friends at the Vagary Bar,
a place more imaginary than real.
    [1. Friendship—Fiction] I. Title.
PZ7.D3877Tw 1981   [Fic]   80-8458
ISBN 0-06-021590-9
ISBN 0-06-021591-7 (lib. bdg.)

Two Blocks Down

PART ONE

1

Happy happy, hummed Star tonelessly. Happy happy. But I'm not really, she thought severely, and frowned. Star was walking the fourteen blocks to school and kicking at the sidewalk. It was swept bare by the hot winds, a long dry stretch of bone. That's what September does to sidewalks.

Happy happy, thought Star insistently. Because I'm young and beautiful, she added, and threw back her head to smile at the sky. She felt September sun on her cheeks and closed her eyes. Happy happy happy.

They were watching her. She could feel their eyes, hotter than the sun on her cheeks. Star sighed. They lived three houses apart, across from hers, and every morning they met on the sidewalk to march up the hill to school. Usually Star left her house as they hit the corner at Vine and Sixth. They'd wait for the light to

1

change, and she would walk slowly, trying not to catch up with them. She always would catch up though, and so they watched her, careful sideways looks under mascara.

So look at me, Star thought, breathing through her teeth, look hard, look again. Star was beautiful. Her mother kept saying so. Truck drivers watched her without embarrassment, and she had trouble meeting the bold eyes of construction workers in the street. Even her mother's Adult Ed students watched her, hiding behind their notebooks. Yes. She was beautiful. No doubt about that. She had her mother's looks, she supposed, except in her mother they were slightly faded and turned inward, dragged at by the years.

"Look," her mother would say on occasion, feeling nostalgic, "here's you, Star. Look. On Harriet Island, that summer." And she would frown a bit, with the album pulled across both their laps, and Star would lean down till her breath fogged the cellophane. That her? Those tiny hands, carefully holding the stick of a melting Dilly Bar, those hands hers? And whose pink coat was she wearing? The thing was, pictures were not real to her. It had to be someone else standing there with ice cream running down her wrist. Star looked at the picture curiously, distantly—it was nothing to do with her. She didn't believe it. But then she could see the dark tangled hair under the pink hood, and the great dark eyes looking warily into the camera, and she thought, Well, maybe. Maybe it was her after all, that summer.

But now. Now, she was sixteen years old, and many

summers had passed since Harriet Island, and she was walking alone to school on a windy September morning. Yes. Things were different now.

Star sighed, yawned, and kicked at a clump of clover on someone's lawn. And from across the street, she finally felt the two pairs of eyes slide off her. Happy happy. Happy.

2

Publicly, Justina Milford and Leslie Armbruster were the best of friends. Privately, they lived on the same block and walked to school together because there was no one else who went their way.

"And," Justina pointed out the first week of school, as she had pointed out every year since seventh grade, "there is a difference between being friends and simply walking to school together."

"Well," said Leslie, "everyone thinks we're friends. I thought we were friends."

"That's not the point. The point is, we're circumstantial friends. Like, if I lived somewhere else, we probably wouldn't get along at all. Don't you see?"

"Oh sure. Look, Just. Are you going to Homecoming this year, do you think? Because if you are, maybe we can—"

"No we couldn't. If you think I'm going to sit in some Italian restaurant and listen to Rick Mausoff have asthma attacks and talk about Fran Tarkenton—"

"I'm not going with him, are you crazy? Lori Sellars told someone that Roddy Mix is going to ask me."

"Well. Sure, Lori. She also told six other girls that Roddy Mix was going to ask them. She's mad about him, you know."

"Look, Just. There's no reason to—"

"There's that girl—look. Don't turn around now, she's watching us."

"Where? I don't see—"

"God, Les. I mean, *god*. When someone says don't turn around, don't turn around. She's in my Brit Lit class. Her name is Star."

"Star what?"

"Who knows? She asked Haugen if we were going to do Chaucer yesterday. Chaucer. We all just looked."

"Well, are you going to?" asked Leslie. They were at school now.

"God, Les! Look—I'll see you at lunch. Lori owes you a ticket. I gave her the one I borrowed from you."

Leslie waved and went to her locker, thinking that Justina was probably right about being circumstantial friends. Because, she thought, twirling the dial to 18-7-3, if I had a choice, I wouldn't pick a friend like Justina Milford. She's really not my type at all.

Leslie stuck her navy-blue windbreaker in the locker, and squinted into a Cracker Jack mirror taped to the door. She'd let Justina cut her bangs last week, because

Justina had a subscription to *Vogue* and knew how they were wearing hair in New York. *Au sauvage,* she had said, waving her scissors savagely, and now Leslie had pale blond strands flopping erratically around her cheeks and nose and getting caught in her eyelashes. She pushed it all back behind her ears and slammed her locker.

"Excuse me," said a voice at her shoulder, "but could you tell me—"

"Oh!" said Leslie, spinning around so that her hair flashed back into her face. "You must be— Well."

"Could you tell me please," said Star, "where the counselor's office is? My schedule seems to be a bit screwed up." Her locker door was open and she leaned against it, shirt lapping at the backs of her knees. Nervously, one long finger fluttered near her cheek.

Well, thought Leslie cautiously, she seems nice enough. A little jumpy, maybe. What could Justina have meant? Star. Bravely, and wishing briefly that her hair didn't look like shit, Leslie smiled brightly. And receiving no reaction from the other girl, smiled again, brighter yet. Leslie had found that a very bright, numbing smile was an extremely handy thing to own, and she used it often.

"Why don't you come with me?" she said finally, "I can show you the way."

"I bet you can," Star said softly, and laughed.

3

"Ma!" Star sang, taking the porch steps three at a time. "I'm home, Mama!" She loped into the kitchen, where her mother sat at the table behind a pile of class evaluation forms, rubbing her eyes. During the day, she was the librarian at the grade school, reading *Curious George* out loud in the voice she used to use with Star. On certain nights, though, she taught Adult Extension in the city—Freelance Marketing at the University, and Structuring the Magazine Article at City Vo-Tech Institute. Occasionally Star accompanied her, sitting in the faculty lounge with a cup of black coffee, or wandering across the campus in the dark. They both enjoyed these occasions and drove home in a comfortable, sleepy silence.

Today, Star kicked through several wads of crushed carbon paper littering the floor, and made a face. "You do make a mess, you know," she remarked, opening the refrigerator. "—*storm is threatenin' my very life today*—what's this Liquid Protein crap?"

"Oh, just nothing. I thought I'd try it, but the taste—So how was school?" She stretched, clasping her head between her elbows, and looked up at Star through eyes that Star recognized as her own. This shocked her every time, and she knew it was the main thing that held them close, this sharing of eyes. "Did you fix your schedule?"

"Yes." Star bit into a chunk of Monterey Jack and swallowed. *"—if I don't get some shelter, oh yeah, I'm gonna fade away—"*

"Star. Don't sing with your mouth full, you'll choke. Remember your cousin Rose—"

"Died with a wishbone up her nose. Ha! This has been going through my head all day. *Gimme, gimme shelter—"*

"Don't, Star. Please. How was school?"

"Not to be believed. They— Well. You know. I got out of Oriental Lit, though, and only have British. They were very nice about it. Kept saying they understood, you know."

"I'm glad."

"I suppose." She wrapped the Monterey Jack in its nest of rumpled Saran, her long fingers moving quickly. "Did you hear from the Institute?"

"Yes, there're eighteen signed up for Group Learning Opportunity, and six independent studies. We start September—let's see here—September ninth."

"Hmm." Star skidded lightly through the carbon paper, on her way to the refrigerator. *"See the fire sweepin' our very street today!"* she sang dramatically.

"Really, Star." Her mother looked at her watch, sighed, and picked up a pen.

"Sorry, Ma. Look, I'm going out for a while. I'll see you at supper, okay?"

"Star—"

" 'Bye, Mama—"

4

Justina and Leslie stood on the sidewalk between their houses, amiably discussing nothing in particular, when Star came flying down her porch steps wearing a hat and Army jacket, face turned to the sky. Reaching the street, she noticed them watching and forcibly slowed herself to a sedate stroll, tucking her hands deeply and decorously into her pockets. She waited until she was well down the street before breaking into a sprint that showed the bottoms of her bare feet.

"Lord," said Justina flatly.

"I think she's kind of neat-looking," said Leslie, arching her neck after Star. "I wouldn't mind terribly if I looked like her."

"But stuck-up," Justina pointed out. "She barely talks. In Brit Lit, we had to interrogate her for ten minutes before she'd tell us where she came from."

"Where?"

"Huh? Oh. I don't know. Somewhere in Minneapolis. I guess her mom wanted to get out of the city, or something like that. She's spacy, that Star."

"I guess so. Hey, Just, guess who asked me to Homecoming today?"

"Rick Mausoff. And he huffed, and he puffed—"

"Cut it out. No. Roddy Mix, and didn't I tell you?"

"But he's practically going with Lori. And besides, he wears false eyelashes."

"He doesn't. You're just jealous."

"Oh lord, Les."

"I'm going to need a dress. God, but I hope my hair grows out before then. Why did I let you cut it?"

"I keep telling you, it looks great. Besides, it's almost like lovely Star's, don't you think?"

"No I don't. I look like John Lennon."

"Well, I could have made you look like Yoko . . ."

"Very funny, Justina."

"Well, I'm sorry. But I'm sick of talking about Roddy Mix, and he does wear false eyelashes, and we're doing Chaucer in Lit, I could vomit."

"Chaucer who? We're doing Huck Finn."

"Sucks. We did it last year, it's all in dialogue—no, not dialogue. What do you call that crap where everyone says 'po-ah' instead of 'poor'?"

"Dialect."

"Yes. Christ. I didn't think I'd come out of that one alive, it's about a million pages long." Justina kicked vigorously at the dirt around the sidewalk. "Look, Les, me and Lori are going to the Mall tomorrow for Homecoming dresses. Come with us, you can get something on sale at Casual Corner."

"Qiana, I suppose," Leslie said thoughtfully, thinking of Huck Finn. She looked up abruptly. "Well. Yes. I'll come."

They parted silently, like old friends, each walking

toward her own house, each knowing the other would be there the next morning. Comfortable, Leslie thought, taking in the newspaper on her porch, familiar. And no longer any need to smile.

5

"After all," said Star to herself, staring grimly into the sandbox in the park, "one has to be alone sometimes." She climbed into the sandbox. "Most of the time, in fact," she amended. The sand was cold, and Star lay back, crossed her legs, and pulled her hat over her eyes. Happy happy, she thought, and felt the sand seeping damply through her jeans.

Ten minutes later, she opened her eyes. I am alone, she thought dramatically, and laughed out loud. "I am ALONE," she said to her hat, and laughed again. She often laughed at herself. She was quite the funniest person she knew.

The narrow wooden side of the sandbox slit her neck, but she didn't move. Half an hour passed, and it was getting dark when Star realized that she wasn't alone in the sandbox. She tilted her hat cautiously off one eye, and looked. It was a little girl with white hair and a grimy ski jacket. She was watching Star. She didn't blink.

"Forgive me for being startled," said Star. "I thought I was alone."

No answer from the little girl.

"Forgive me for being rude," said Star, "but can you talk? I mean, when do kids start talking lately?"

No answer.

"Probably you're exceptionally bright," said Star conversationally. "Exceptionally bright people quite often don't talk till much later, you know. Albert Schweitzer, for instance."

Silence.

"On the other hand, of course," said Star, "you could simply be stupid."

"Stupid," said the little girl.

"Yes," said Star. She rolled over on her stomach. "The reason I was startled was, every time I open my eyes, I'm looking for someone. But I never see anyone. Do you see?"

"Stupid," said the little girl.

"Stupid stupid," said Star listlessly. "You start early, don't you?"

"Stupid," agreed the little girl. She picked up a handful of sand and stuffed it into the pocket of her jacket.

"Oh really," said Star, frowning, "I don't think I'd do that if I were you."

"Stupid," glared the little girl. She tipped her head to look at Star. Star looked back calmly. The little girl scooped more sand and filled the other pocket.

"On the other hand, of course," said Star, "I'm not

you." She stood up and scraped sand off her jeans. It stuck to her hands. "I'm leaving now." She slung her hat on her head, and watched the wind ruffle the girl's white hair. She put her hand on the girl's head. The girl looked up with a frown.

"What ho for the life of a bear!" sang Star, and laughed. She climbed out of the sandbox and turned into the twilight. Heading home. At the park gate, she looked back quickly. Yes, the girl was still there, standing white-haired in the gloom. "Sing ho!" shouted Star, going through the gate. "Sing ho for the life of a bear!"

Going home that night, Star was happy.

6

"—said it would cost me fifteen dollars if I got it done anywhere else. So I did it right there." Leslie was trudging along behind the Hoover and screaming above the roar.

"Well," screamed back Justina, who was trudging along behind Leslie and swiping at the air with a dustcloth, "I still like it the way I cut it better."

"I've always wanted it short, you know," shouted Leslie, "but Mom wouldn't let me get it cut. Until you chopped it, you know. Then she figured anything was better."

"You've neither of you got any taste. I keep telling you, *Vogue* says unruly is *in*."

"Unruly! Justina, what you did to my head was unholy. God." Leslie flipped the switch, and the Hoover died a slow death. She peered into the mirror above the electric fireplace, and made a face. "Oh geez—my eyes stick out. Have you ever noticed that?"

"Yeah. A little bit. Not much."

"Oh god. Why didn't you say anything?"

"You couldn't tell with the haircut I gave you. Couldn't even see your eyes."

"Are you hungry?" asked Leslie, turning away from the mirror.

"Yes—" Justina tossed her dustcloth and followed Leslie into the kitchen. Leslie put a plate of Swedish meatballs in the microwave and sat on the dryer to wait.

"Say, Justina," she said. She cleared her throat and pulled at her earring. It was her birthstone, and a present from Justina in ninth grade. Two pairs for a dollar fifty, and Justina had gotten her own birthstone at the same time. "You know that girl across the street?"

"Oh lord," said Justina. "What about her? She fell asleep in Lit day before yesterday. All hour. Just nodded off behind her notebook. We all just sat and looked. I mean— Lord."

"Well. Lots of people sleep in school."

"No," said Justina, "they don't. It's very hard to sleep in school. I mean, sure, you can put your head down, and maybe doze off if you're lucky. But this kid was really *out.* And she comes staggering in late every day, with her eyes all wild and shirt all sticking out in back—Lord. She's a mess."

"Well," said Leslie. *Ping* went the timer on the microwave. She removed the meatballs. "Well. She lives right across the street, you know."

"Don't tell me you want to make a social call on her. Where's the—oh. Thanks. Do you have Tabasco—never mind. This is fine. Look, Les. Some people you just stay away from, you know? Well, she's one of them."

"I guess so. But—oh. I forgot to tell you. Roddy Mix says that if you don't have a date for Homecoming, he's got this friend in Stillwater—"

"What makes Roddy Mix think I need his friends to get a date? Honestly. Besides, I've seen his Stillwater friends and they don't exactly drive you mad with desire. Acne down to their ankles, most of them. And all with those eyelashes."

"Oh come on, Just. This one's name is Derek, and he works at that Honda place over at the Mall. He's okay. Really. See, and then we could double—"

"Derek? And the Dominoes? Really, Les, I don't want to sound churlish—"

"Oh come on, Justina. Anyway, you don't have to tell me now. Roddy says he can wait. Do you want any more of this stuff?"

"Mmm. Just the sauce. There. Thanks."

Leslie carried the leftover meatballs to the refrigerator, dripping sauce along the way. She stood in front of Justina and fingered her hair. It was alarmingly short. She was miserable. "I've got to finish with the Hoover,"

14

she said to Justina, "before Mom gets home."

"Mmm," said Justina, standing up, "I'm just leaving." She flicked her sleeve across her face and picked up her jacket, which was draped across the ironing board.

"See you, Les," she said cheerfully, and went out whistling.

Alone, Leslie carefully wiped the sauce from the dryer. She touched her hair and sighed. Where was the vacuum cleaner? She reached for the handle and stood over the Hoover, poised like James Bond. Then she shook herself and flipped the switch.

"Honestly," she said severely, over the roar, "anyone would think I was unstable."

7

Room 312, the University. Star entered the room humming, a bit winded from the stairs, and carrying her mother's briefcase and the attendance folder. She kicked the doorstop into place and walked to the long table. *Plonk.* Briefcase at the head, followed by the folder. Eighteen heads flew up at the plonk, and eighteen pairs of eyes flew to Star's face. Half to laugh. She coughed and smiled. "She'll be here in a minute. Elevator's slow tonight."

In the hall she met her mother. "They're waiting anxiously, Ma."

"Yes—darling, what are you going to do with yourself tonight?"

"Oh! Don't worry about me. I'll be fine. Can I have a dollar?"

"I don't think I have any change. Look, if you go downtown, be careful. There're odd people around. Don't talk to anyone."

"I won't."

"And be at the car by ten o'clock. If you're not there, Star, I wouldn't know where to look for you. I mean it."

"I know. I'll be there."

"And Star. Could you stop at Shinder's and get me a new *Charlotte's Web*, please? Here. Don't lose the change."

"Yeah. I won't. Good-bye." How her mother went on! It was like this every week, as if she was still that tiny thing in a pink hood on Harriet Island. And so little time. Star stood on restless feet in front of the elevator, despaired, and bolted for the stairway. Down she flew, eyes wide, past the janitor leaning on a mop, out the door. Into the cool twilight, into a wind that lifted the hair off her face. Lights glaring and blinking, cars shrieking, steam spiraling above the sewers. Star loved the city, she felt closer to herself in the city. Before, living here, it had been easy, almost too easy. Every night, calmly, she'd put a pile of books under her arm— "The library again?" her mother would say, shaking her head fondly, but Star would only shrug and smile. Once out the door, the books would be tucked under a mailbox, and Star was on her own. West Bank, Dinkytown, downtown, uptown, she knew and loved them all. Sometimes she just caught a bus and rode for hours, making up epics about the people she saw. Alone. But alone, she was never lonely, ever.

Star pulled her sweaters around her and pounded her heels into the sidewalk. It was different now, of course. She smiled. Coming home from the U one night, her mother had stopped to mail her subscription renewal to *Booklist*, and had found Star's pile of books underneath the box, damp and spotted from the dew. It was decided that a smaller-town environment would do wonders for them both. "Think of it, Star! Every night, I could cross the bridge home, and be out of this hot city. Think what it will do for my blood pressure."

Yes. So there they were. But Star didn't mind, not really, it didn't make that much difference where she was as long as she could be alone in her head. And besides, there was always Thursday night. She pushed her hands into her pockets, breathed in deeply, and smiled at two ladies with Woolworth's shopping bags. They looked hastily at their feet. She giggled.

Three blocks later, she stalked into Shinder's. Found *Charlotte's Web*. Then she sat on a pile of inky tabloids and read *Rolling Stone* cover to cover, noticing, as she thumbed the pages, that the store windows were filling with darkness. Just about seven o'clock. She got to her feet, paid for Charlotte, and returned to the street. A

DONT WALK sign flashed red, and she rocked gently on her heels on the curb.

"I am alone," she intoned, "I am all alone." The light changed. Star crossed the street, and cars idled impatiently at the corner. "Alone alone," she hummed aimlessly.

Two blocks down and one over, watching herself in the store windows and singing. "Lovely lovely, all alone." She was in an alley. Shadows mixed gracefully with garbage cans and clotheslines, and Star climbed a rickety porch and pounded a door. A flowerpot crashed at her feet. She frowned. "Alone alone," she hummed disapprovingly, and kicked the flowerpot into the shadows.

"Who's there?" said the door. Star sighed.

"It's me, Star. Open up."

"Star!" The door lunged open, and Star leaped out of the way. "Honey, we just about gave up on you! Nicky even put your mug away, but I knew you'd be back—but where have you been?"

"My mother's semester started tonight," said Star, climbing into a dimly lit room. "It's the only time I can get into the city now, you know. Also," she added, tossing *Charlotte's Web* into an enormous wok standing decoratively by the door, "school started last week. There's always a mess with that."

"School. Are you still going to school?"

"I'm sixteen, Connie. Do you have any apricot brandy for me?"

"It seems to me that you've been going to school

18

forever. I should think you'd— Well, I'll go out front and check for the brandy. God, but it's good to see you back. The others will—"

Star settled back against a pile of pillows stacked along one wall, and smiled dreamily to herself. She was in the back room of the Vagary Bar. Its occupants she knew by first name only, but she considered them her best friends, and they in turn treated her with an amused paternalism she found comforting. Star never felt lonely at the Vagary Bar.

The small door which led to the main bar flew open, letting in a burst of smoky air and the jangling of pinballs. Star sighed. This would be Nicky, preceded by his teeth. "Hi there, Nick," she called, struggling off the pillows.

"Star!" Nicky was long-legged, long-armed, and long-toothed, and he stood in the doorway with two bottles of brandy, grinning. He was the editor of an underground paper at the U, called the *Prick*, but you couldn't tell to look at him. He flung his arms around Star, and the brandy bottles crashed together behind her back. "Where have you been, dear girl? Is life so fulfilling in the suburbs that you can't waste a minute to come round and visit the family?"

"For sure. No, Nicky, you know the semester starts tonight."

"Ah, yes. Freelance Marketing. Do you know, Star, I might just enroll in your mama's class sometime? Some of the stuff I've been turning out in *Prick*—"

"Don't you try it, Nicky dear. I can just see that."

19

"Now, don't get upset, love, I was merely joshing. Now here. Have some of this, and tell me what's new in your little life."

"Thank you. Nothing."

"Oh, Star, Star. If you'd only let me photograph you for the *Prick*—I can see it now. A full-page spread with you in some Victorian costume, flowers in your hair, the whole bit, and a caption. 'Life in Finishing School' or wait—I've got it. 'Young Blood.' You like that?"

"I'd have to be pretty desperate before I'd think of doing that, Nick."

Connie stepped into the room with a case of empties and a girl. The girl was in an elaborate felt hat. She flipped her eyelashes at Star. Star looked at the ceiling.

"Nicky," said Connie, "you'd better get out front. There's a fellow what wants a Pimm's Number One."

"Chappie in gold lamé?" said Nicky, stuffing his arms and legs out the door. "Yes. I remember him and his Pimm's. Think about my spread, won't you, Star?"

Felt hat slunk over to the pile of pillows and smiled down at Star. "I thought we'd seen the last of you, Starbaby. We were getting a bit alarmed, you know. But then, no one leaves the Vagary Bar, do they?"

"Aw, Meggie. It's nice that you were so concerned. But you know how it is—school and my mother." Star walked to the stereo in a corner, surrounded by flowerpots and empty bottles and sitting on a rickety Queen Anne table. She punched a few buttons and made a face. Muddy Waters. "How do you listen to that, Meggie? It puts me into a coma."

"Quite the sophisticate, aren't we? I don't care. Change it. Your stuff is on the shelf. Where Alec's used to be."

"What happened to Alec?" asked Star, flipping through a stack of records. She found the Rolling Stones' *Big Hits*, and put a record on over Muddy Waters. Meggie groaned.

"Alec is in Salt Lake City, trying to be a Mormon. He turned pious in June, and went west in July."

"What happened to his Kawasaki?" said Star, putting her head on her knees and humming along gently with the Stones.

"Gave it to Nick. He renounced all his material possessions. He'll be back. I give him six weeks, tops. A Mormon, indeed. Was just yesterday he was selling watered-down vermouth to the suburban sixth graders."

Star giggled. She put her glass of brandy on the floor, and curled up on a rug next to the stereo. Electric guitars and static flashed over her head. She closed her eyes. Meggie stood up languidly, crossed the room, and put her hand on Star's head. She wrapped long, red-tipped fingers in Star's tangled hair. Her eyes glinted under the felt hat. Ten minutes passed noiselessly.

"Meggie," Star whispered, muffled from the rug.

"Yes, Star-baby," whispered Meggie, leaning down expectantly.

"Wake me up before ten o'clock please. My mother wouldn't know where to look."

8

" 'I have y-seen segges, quod he,' " read Justina in a loud, bored voice. She cleared her throat and wrapped a piece of hair around her finger. " 'In the cite of London beren beighes ful brighte abouten here nekkes—' "

"Thank you, Justina. Now, what does that mean?"

"Hmm," Justina said, scanning the page. She sighed. She looked hard at her feet. "Well. He thinks— Well."

Snickers from the class. Justina arched her eyebrows and looked at Miss Haugen.

"Thank you, Justina. Now in this passage, the author—yes, Star?"

"He has seen creatures in the city of London," said Star, rubbing her eyes and blinking, "wearing bright collars around their necks." She settled back in her chair.

"Lord," said Justina distinctly. More snickers.

"Well," said Miss Haugen, who had planned to spend the entire hour translating. "Well then." She looked bleakly at the clock.

Justina smoothed her hair and looked at her fingernails. Coral Pink looked fine in the bathroom, but it lost something in fluorescence. She looked around the room at Star, who had her cheek propped on her hand and hair in her eyes. She was wearing a New York

City Ballet T-shirt, and gray military pants with a rip down one thigh. Lord, thought Justina disapprovingly, and wondered if her own mother would let her leave the house dressed like that. Probably not. She looked closer. Star's eyelashes made shadows on her cheeks. She was dozing. Lord, thought Justina again, and pulled a pen delicately from the hip pocket of her tan corduroys.

"Who IS that kid??" she wrote gently in the palm of her hand, and flashed it across the aisle at Roddy Mix, who closed his lashes briefly over blue eyes. There was something about Roddy Mix that bothered Justina, but she had neither the ambition nor the articulation to mention it out loud. She recognized that he was male, and almost excessively good-looking, but sometimes it made her uncomfortable to look at him. Sometimes she felt his eyes in her back like bright needle points, but when she turned uneasily to look at him, he would be smiling sleepily to himself.

On the other hand, of course, Justina was inclined to be romantic about things like that. Again, she flashed her palm at Roddy Mix, who leaned forward slightly to read it this time.

" 'Men myghte wite where thei went, and awei renne!' " read Miss Haugen, with one eye on the clock. Nine-twenty-six.

"Who is that kid," Roddy Mix echoed thoughtfully, rather loudly. "Well I don't know. But she's gorgeous, don't you think?"

Star's eyelashes jerked off her cheeks as if she'd been shot, and Justina frowned.

23

" 'To bugge a belle of brasse or of brighte sylver,' "
said Miss Haugen loudly, " 'And knitten on a colere
for owre commune profit.' "

"She isn't much," sniffed Justina in a whisper.

"Write," said Roddy Mix, "Haugen's looking."

"She's a witch," whispered Justina, ignoring him.
"Both of them." She scraped at her nail polish with
the spiral on her notebook and hoped Leslie had a lunch
ticket she could borrow. Twenty minutes till the bell.
"What's for lunch?" she penned on her other palm,
and flashed it across the aisle.

"Hot dogs and fruit cup," he scrawled on the cover
of his Lit book. Justina sighed.

" 'That dorst have y-bounden the belle aboute the
cattis nekke,' " read Miss Haugen triumphantly, and
clapped the book shut.

9

Happy happy, thought Star listlessly. She was sitting in
the school library at lunch. *Soviet Life* magazine was open
on her knees and she turned the pages mechanically.
Putting her head on her shoulder, she glared at a peasant
in a babushka. Nicky had a scarf like that. Happy happy
happy.

Ten minutes later, she felt someone shake her tentatively by one shoulder. She blinked and looked up at a blue-eyed boy with curiously long eyelashes. "Hello," she said uncertainly, and squinted. He looked familiar. She laughed. "Do I know you?"

"I—no, I sit three seats up in Brit Lit. My name is—uh—Roddy Mix."

"Of course," said Star gravely, and laughed again. Really, she thought.

"I didn't mean to bother you, but—well, the bell just rang. You'll be late for fifth hour if you don't hurry."

"Oh," said Star, unfolding her legs. "Yes. I suppose so." She put *Soviet Life* neatly on the shelf and turned around to smile at the boy. "I must have dozed off."

"You seem to do that quite a lot," said Roddy Mix, and blushed.

"Do I really?" Star remarked absently, pushing hair off her face. "I suppose I do. Yes. Must be the air. Well. Thank you, Ronnie."

"Roddy. You're welcome. I hope I didn't interrupt anything."

Star laughed and shook her head. "No." She picked up her notebooks, which were scattered limply around the chair. "Certainly not," she added, tucking the back of her shirt into gray flannel. Looking down, she noticed that there seemed to be a long rip down one thigh. Funny she hadn't noticed before. "Well—"

The boy certainly looked familiar. She walked slowly toward the library door. At the door, she stopped and looked very hard at the doorknob. Who? She shook her head.

"Come back," said Roddy Mix softly.

Star hesitated. "Why?" she asked. Still facing the door. But it didn't matter; looking up, she saw him reflected in the display case, at her shoulder. "What do you want?" she said, a bit desperately. She wasn't at all used to having people stand this close.

"You don't like it here, do you?" He was amazing himself, talking like this to someone he didn't know, but he couldn't stop, it kept coming.

Alec? Star said nothing.

"You don't like it anywhere, do you?" He didn't know this, he was just guessing, but he saw the pulse leap in her neck and knew he was right. But the discovery only made him suddenly uncomfortable, he wished he hadn't started this. Too late. She stood there, hand on the doorknob, fragile and fierce. He wanted to say something gentle, something suave, he wanted to touch her, he wanted—

But Star laughed. She tossed her hair back and looked at him scornfully. "Do you really want an answer to that, Ronnie?"

"Roddy," he said automatically, but she was out the door then, and he stood under the fluorescent lights, blinking.

10

"I want to meet her," said Justina flatly. She was in Leslie's bedroom, and doing Chemistry homework underneath Peter Frampton's 23″ × 35″ smile.

"But why?" asked Leslie. Mass equals volume times density.

"Because," said Justina, glaring at Peter. "I do. And Roddy Mix thinks she's gorgeous."

"He does?" Leslie laid her pencil down, and looked suspiciously at Justina. "Oh, he does not. You're making that up. I know you, Just."

"For godssake, Les, why would I make that up? Anyway, it doesn't matter. It's just that she lives across the street, you know. Right across the street."

"I told you that before. Look, Just. What did Roddy Mix say?"

"Oh nothing. You know. But I thought we'd just go over and introduce ourselves."

"I suppose. What did you get for number eight?"

"Point six grams. We'll go, then? You'll come with me?"

"Yes— Justina, they want the answer in grams per liter. It's a density problem."

27

"Oh shit. I did all of these wrong, then. Is it mass times volume, or what?"

"Density equals mass over volume. Look, Just, what did Roddy say about her?"

"Lord, Les. I can't remember. Haugen was reading on and on about some brass or something. Cat's neck— I don't know. Real crap. Look. Did you get fourteen point six grams per liter for number one?"

"Mmm. Yeah. It sounds awkward, going over like this. I mean, she's been across the street for—what?— four months, and we come strolling over out of the blue—what'll she think?"

"Who knows? She's spacy, she'll never notice. Say, Les, do you have any of those Swedish meatballs left?"

"Yes. Eight point six nine five seven for number three. Do you want me to go down?"

"If you wouldn't mind."

Leslie stood up and went downstairs with her pencil hanging from the corner of her mouth. Justina gazed thoughtfully into Peter Frampton's eyes, and said "spacy" to herself. Then she shook her head, and copied Leslie's Chemistry answers neatly into her own notebook.

"Yes," she said out loud once more, "spacy."

11

"Six independent studies at thirty-seven sixty per person," remarked Star's mother, sitting cross-legged at the kitchen table, "that's—let's see here—that's two twenty-five sixty. Not bad, wouldn't you say?"

"Gorgeous," agreed Star. Her bathrobe was wrapped around her twice, and a cup of nutmeg-spiked coffee stood in front of her. "Of course," she added, "those in class pay more."

"Yes, but they're such a—" Star's mother stopped, and lifted her coffee cup to her mouth. "About class, Star. I was thinking about you and those Thursday nights. Don't you ever get bored, waiting around for class to end? I mean, three hours of wandering about with nothing to do is not my idea of fun."

"Well, Mama, what's fun? It's just where you find it, you know."

"Oh Star." She leaned across the table and patted Star's terry-cloth shoulder. "Sometimes I worry about you, honey. You always seem to be so—so by yourself."

"I am alone," Star intoned, and laughed. "Don't worry about me, Ma. I find things. Yes, I do." She picked at the lace on the tablecloth. *"Just a shot away, it's just a shot away . . ."*

"Oh Star. Honestly."

Star stood up and walked to the window. Leaves swirled in the dark, and rattled in the roof gutters. The wind howled. Star leaned on her elbows and propped her chin against the glass. Then she started singing, quietly this time. *"Oh a storm is threatnin' my very life today, if I don't get some shelter . . ."*

"Star—those two girls across the street."

"What about them? *Rape! Murder! It's just a shot away!"*

"Do you think that maybe they look—well, okay? Like, maybe you'd like them?"

"Not likely," said Star, giving the matter very little thought. She moved away from the window. Happy happy. "Umm—I don't know what I like, Ma. I know what I don't like. You know what I don't like."

"Oh, honey. You don't like curling irons, you don't like the smell of mimeograph ink, and you don't like Peter Frampton. What does that mean?"

"What does it all mean, Alfie?" hummed Star, and blew her mother a kiss as she left the kitchen.

She climbed the back steps and stood in the doorway of her room. Star loved her room. It was small and dark, with a slanted ceiling and stacks of secondhand paperbacks lining the walls. A four-poster bed stood near the window with Star's hat collection hanging from the posts. She had covered all four walls with magazine covers, and was surrounded by slick, gleaming celebrity smiles. It used to make her uneasy to undress in front of Rudolf Nureyev's *Saturday Review* smirk, and Bianca Jagger's eyes were definitely unnerving on *Viva*, but

30

Star had gotten used to that. She smiled at her *Cosmo* girls, turned off her light, and switched on her radio. It was kept at a progressive sort of FM station because the dreary, psychedelic, eleven-minute guitar solos worked like Valium on her.

Star slipped a sheepskin vest over her bathrobe, and put a pair of sweat socks on her feet. She curled up in her pillows, and the Grateful Dead pounded harmlessly over her head. Happy happy, she thought drowsily, and went to sleep.

12

Actually, the Homecoming Dance had gone rather well at first, Leslie thought. This year's decorating committee, with a few recruits from Art II, had outdone last year's, and the gym was violently bedecked in orange and mauve. It was all very exciting, Leslie thought, until she fell out of her shoe. And shrieked.

"Ohmygod," whispered Roddy Mix, watching, unable to move in his morbid fascination. "Oh, god . . ."

"Look," said Leslie, through closed teeth, "I'm all right. I just fell out of my shoe is all." The shoes were new, and her mother had warned her but of course she hadn't listened, and her mother would be glad.

"Well—" Roddy Mix said, looking around the gym desperately. "Can I—do you want some punch, Leslie?"

"Yes," breathed Leslie, trying hard to smile graciously. "Please, Roddy." She limped to the row of bleachers along one wall, and sat gingerly with crossed legs. Already she could see her ankle swelling relentlessly against her new Rosy Suntan nylons. Roddy Mix headed eagerly for the refreshment table.

"Les!" Leslie turned her head, and Justina was beside her, wearing apple-green Qiana with a scrubbed-at dribble of taco sauce on one shoulder. Behind her stood a pale boy wearing a shirt with the Honda insignia over the pocket under his dinner jacket.

"Lord, Les!" boomed Justina. "What happened? Where's Roddy Mix?"

"I fell out of my shoe. He's getting punch. You've got taco sauce on your shoulder."

"I know it. My corsage fell off on the way over. Look Les, are you okay?"

"No, I'm not. Is that Derek?"

"Yes. We'll talk about him later."

"Pleased to meetcher," Derek said, stepping forward.

Justina brushed him aside, her face yellowish with concern above apple-green Qiana. "Do you want to go home, Les? Because if you do, I'll track down Roddy Mix and—"

"I can't—" Leslie stopped and sighed. She was beginning to feel weary of the whole evening, and thought briefly and wistfully of her pale-blue and white bedroom under Peter Frampton's 23″ × 35″ smile. On the gym floor, couples moved awkwardly to the music, unfamiliar in Sunday clothes, and Leslie turned away. She reached

32

down to ease the shoe off her swollen foot, tugging at the heel.

Justina pulled at the neck of her dress and said, "We could go home if you wanted to, Les. I mean, it's not too early, if that's what you're worried about."

The shoe wouldn't move. Leslie could feel it scraping against Rosy Suntan nylon, and pressing on a small blister near her arch. She slid her thumb under the strap and wrenched. The shoe left her foot and clattered on the wooden bleacher seat before falling ten feet to the floor below. "Shit," said Leslie, and sighed. She wasn't surprised.

"Oh lord, Les—" Justina looked around. "Lord. Here comes Roddy."

"I could only get water, Leslie," said Roddy Mix, handing her a paper cup. "There's a real mess at the refreshment table."

"That's fine. Roddy, you're not going to believe this, but my shoe—"

"I could go back and stand in line if you want me to."

"What? Oh. No, that's okay, Roddy, Really. Water's fine. But Roddy—my shoe, it kind of fell through the bleachers, and I'd really appreciate—"

"No, it's okay, Leslie. I don't mind standing in line. I don't even think the water's cold. Here, give me the cup."

"Roddy, I—"

"Look," said Justina, stepping forward. She put her hands on apple-green hips. "Her shoe fell through the

33

bleachers. Are you going to do something about it, or do I get a chaperone?"

"Oh, Justina!" Leslie wailed, and wished she was dead. She smiled bleakly at Roddy.

"Well," said Roddy Mix, and blinked. His neatly brushed hair started to curl around his ears. He looked at the ceiling, where orange streamers fluttered gently heavenward. "Tame the Tigers," they said.

"All you have to do," Justina explained patiently, "is walk underneath and find it."

"I'll go," offered Derek suddenly, from behind Justina's shoulder. They stared. "Really," he added, "I'm used to it."

"Used to it," echoed Justina blankly. "Well. That's nice of you, Derek. Look, it's right underneath. A little to the left, you'll see it right away."

"Right away," echoed Roddy Mix, and scratched his nose. The band swung into "Stairway to Heaven." The couples went to the center of the gym like moths, and Justina stationed herself at a crack between bleacher seats.

"Do you see him?" Leslie asked, swinging her foot.

"No. He must be—oh, there he is!" Justina pressed her face to the crack. "Derek!" she shouted. "Over here."

"She's got taco sauce on her shoulder," Roddy Mix remarked to Leslie.

"Her corsage fell off," Leslie said. She felt for some reason very tired, even though it couldn't have been much later than eleven. It was the effort, she supposed.

All evening she had felt herself being charming, had heard her gay giddy laughter, felt her bright brittle smile. It was wearing, and she didn't have the stamina.

"Oh, Roddy," said Leslie suddenly, without thinking, "I'm so sorry."

He looked down at her, his eyes empty and blue. Leslie marveled silently at his lashes. "That's all right, Leslie," he said. "It wasn't your fault, really. Some of those shoes are deadly."

"No, I mean—" She tried to look at him, but his thoughts were somewhere else. She sighed. "I just mean, I'm afraid I'm not very good company now. It's hard to keep that sort of thing up, you know."

He smiled then, and said, "I like you better like this, Leslie."

"You do?" Maybe the evening wasn't wrecked after all.

"Yeah." He sucked in his cheeks and looked at the ceiling again. "I like people who always act like they do when they're alone. Who don't change for people all the time. Do you know what I mean?"

"Oh yes," Leslie breathed, even though she didn't.

"There are people like that, you know." He stopped talking. He's not mad, thought Leslie, and smiled brightly. Roddy turned his head. "But those people," he said, "will never let you know them."

Leslie had nothing to say to this. She wondered briefly whom he was referring to—Justina? Probably not, he wasn't too fond of Justina. She thought some more, but then there was a triumphant cry from the bleachers, and Justina was coming toward them, waving Leslie's shoe aloft as if claiming territory for the U.S.A. One small step for mankind, thought Leslie bleakly.

"Here it is, Les," said Justina. "How are you feeling?"

"I don't know," Leslie answered. "Actually, I'd kind of like to go home—that is, if you don't mind—"

"Right," Justina said, taking charge. "Roddy! Hey. Roddy Mix."

"I'm right here," Roddy said. "Did he find it?"

"Yes. Look, Roddy, I want you to take us home. Now."

"Now? But we thought—" He looked at the bleachers, where Derek was picking his way toward them slowly. "Well, we thought we'd go out and have a few—"

"Roddy. Shut up. We want to go home," said Justina loudly. She grabbed Leslie by one wrist, and pulled her to her feet. Leslie blushed. "Now."

"I can wait, Justina," Leslie whispered. "Really. I don't mind."

"Shut up, Les." Justina stalked across the gym with Leslie limping along behind in one shoe, and Derek followed placidly, swinging Leslie's other shoe by one strap. And bringing up the rear was Roddy Mix, hands in pockets, hair shining smoothly, whistling tonelessly to himself.

There was silence in the car on the way home, made much worse by the discovery that Roddy's radio wouldn't work. Separately, the four of them hummed top-40 tunes to themselves, hoping to mask the relentless

36

quiet. Ten minutes later, they arrived at Leslie's house in great relief.

"That's fine," Justina said from the backseat. "You don't have to come in." No one moved. Across the street a light shone softly on the front porch of Star's house. She was lounging in a hammock, her hair a halo around her head, and a paperback open across blanket-wrapped knees. Hearing Roddy's car, she looked up slowly, and her profile was sharp against the darkness. In the car three pairs of eyes watched, fascinated—Derek was too busy groping at Justina to bother. Minutes passed. And then Star's mouth widened in a maliciously amused smile, as casually she reached up to switch off the porch light.

"Lord," said Justina flatly as she struggled out of the backseat, her apple-green Qiana looking considerably less fresh than it had at eight. "Knock it off," she added to Derek, scowling into the car.

"Well," said Leslie bravely. "Thank you for a nice time, Roddy."

Roddy Mix sat watching the dark front porch across the street. His fingers were locked across the steering wheel.

"I did enjoy myself," Leslie continued, louder. "Really." She took a breath, and pushed her face into the night's last dazzling smile.

"Oh," said Roddy Mix, and blinked. "Did you really, Leslie? Well. I'm glad." And he smiled politely and drove away, humming something that sounded like "Stairway to Heaven."

13

Star sat forlornly in the far corner of the Vagary Bar. The room was dark, and dust hung all around, and Star was sharply conscious of sitting forlornly in a lonely room. She knew, however, that loneliness wouldn't last long. She smiled and closed her eyes.

"Listen to the night noises," she said softly. "It sounds like winter, Nicky."

"Don't get lyrical with me, love," said Nicky, raising a Heineken to his mouth. "Now. I want you to listen to this, it's an editorial I wrote. Okay. 'A matter of great concern to any member of the—' "

" 'For when thy labour doon al is,' " mumbled Star through her knees, " 'And hast y-maad thy reken-ings—' "

"—how far do those pigs think they can go? For every student who is not receiving any form of financial aid, there are at least twelve—"

" 'And, also domb as any stoon,' " said Star to herself. The back room of the Vagary Bar was all warm gold light and shadows, and Star felt languid and peaceful. Reality was far away, and everything that existed was right here under her eyelashes. No one was here who didn't belong. It was safe in the Vagary Bar, safe and warm, and Muddy Waters' voice spilled liquidly over the clinking of glasses. Star sighed. " 'Thou sittest at another boke,' " she murmured.

Meggie, slinky under velvet turban and satin flowers, appeared at Star's right shoulder. " 'Till fully dawsed is thy loke, and livest thous as a hermyte, although thine abstinence is lyte.' "

"Oh," said Star, jumping a little. "Meggie. You scared me."

"Is your abstinence light, Star-baby?" asked Meggie. She sat in a white wicker chair with her legs crossed cynically. Removing an ivory cigarette holder from her folds of velvet, she lit up and squinted lazily through the smoke. "Well?"

"Oh Meggie, don't be silly. I'm not abstaining from anything. In fact," she added, breathing in gently, "I'm quite happy."

"Of course you're happy here, Star-baby. But how often are you here, after all?"

"As often as I need to be," said Star. She got off the floor, brushed at the seat of her pants, and sat down at the wicker table across from Meggie. Between them, a half-finished jigsaw puzzle lay limply, with curling dusty edges. Star noticed idly that it seemed to be half of the London Bridge. She placed her elbows carefully over a patch of the Thames, and leaned forward. Hair fell in her mouth. "Have you heard from Alec lately?"

"Yes. He's coming back, exactly as I said he would. Connie says he can have his job back, and Nicky's returning the Kawasaki. Alec—he's always running off like that, you know, and it's back to the Vagary Bar one month later."

"That's kind of nice."

"Oh Star-baby, it's not nice at all. There is really no leaving this place."

"For some people." Star pulled at a strand of wicker at the edge of the table. It occurred to her that she might unravel the entire table and send it collapsing to the floor, so she stopped. The loose strand at the edge bothered her, and she tried not to look at it.

"I don't know about that," said Meggie. "But it doesn't much matter. I'm going to love seeing Alec again."

"This boy in my school reminds me of Alec. He's got those eyelashes, and he walks just like Alec. You really wouldn't believe it."

"What boy?" asked Meggie, pulling casually on her ivory holder.

"Oh. I don't know. His name is Ronnie something. Roddy. He's in my British Lit class."

"Do you like him?" Meggie scratched her knee, thoughtfully.

"Oh Meggie, really. He's going with one of those horrible feather-hair girls with the imitation turquoise rings, you know. Leslie somebody. She lives across the street."

"Hmm," said Meggie, and shrugged. " 'Allas, that swich a cas me sholde falle!' "

"For sure," laughed Star. She lifted her elbows off

40

the Thames, and pieces stuck to her skin. "Where's this thing from?" she asked.

"Alec started it before he left. Nobody knows why. It's just been sitting here, getting dusty, and Connie won't touch it because she knows he'll be coming back. Just like she wouldn't touch your precious Stones."

"If you do," sang Star in a deep voice, *"I'll stick my knife right down your throat, yeah!"*

"It's nine-fifteen," said Meggie. Star stood up, ran over to say good-bye to Nicky, who was reading his editorial to three sleeping girls, and headed for the cold alley. Meggie stood by the door, and her satin flowers flapped in the wind.

"What's the last line, Meggie?" shouted Star, with hair in her mouth, and her eyes full of laughter. "Tell me the last line, Meggie!"

"And it hurts," said Meggie softly.

"What?"

"And it hurts," bellowed Meggie. Star grinned and waved, and Meggie backed into the Vagary Bar smiling.

14

"Where did Chaucer spend his early boyhood?" asked Miss Haugen in her test voice.

Justina crossed her legs delicately and looked hard at her feet, where a few pertinent facts concerning Geoffrey Chaucer were penned on the sides of her shoes. Lori Sellars had had the test first hour, and Justina was prepared. "Westminster," she wrote neatly behind an equally neat number 1.

"Who were the king and queen at the time of Chaucer's French influence?" read Miss Haugen distinctly, and checked her lipstick in the face of her wristwatch.

Lord, thought Justina, scanning her shoe. Lori had not said anything about kings and queens. She slid her eyes thoughtfully to the ceiling, and looked at Roddy Mix's paper on the way up. He had no answer for the second question and something that looked like Racine, Wisconsin, for the first. Justina frowned.

"Edward and Mary," she wrote not so neatly, and stretched. On the way down, she noted that Star had her hair pulled back into a messy knot, and was reading *Rolling Stone* under her desk. Justina sniffed disdainfully.

"Which of Chaucer's poems are autobiographical?" enunciated Miss Haugen with a veiled look at the clock.

Justina brought her left leg up and laid the ankle over her right knee. This answer had extended all the way to the sole. "Leg. G. Wom.," she read, and frowned. She stared boldly at Roddy Mix. He was drawing footballs in his margins and didn't notice her. She tucked her plaid flannel shirt into the waistband of blue corduroys, and cleared her throat. Roddy Mix lifted his head and rubbed his eyes with the back of his wrist.

"Leg. G. Wom.," Justina scrawled, using three lines on her paper. Three seats back, she heard Star flipping the pages of *Rolling Stone.*

"Where was Chaucer buried?" asked Miss Haugen, and coughed delicately into her peach polyester sleeve.

Help, thought Justina distinctly, and lifted the cover of her Lit notebook. Buried buried buried, she said to herself with one eye on Miss Haugen. San Benett? St. Benete? St. Benet. You're clever, Justina Milford, she said to herself, and a smile sliced her cheeks.

"St. Benet Chapel," she printed carefully. Across the aisle, Roddy Mix yawned and stuck his legs into the aisle. He folded his arms across his chest, with his pencil hanging under his elbow like a cigar, and looked sideways at Star. Justina, who didn't miss much in the way of classroom drama, looked on and frowned. She placed her elbow gently on the desk behind her and swung her head around smoothly. Star, who was unaware of the attention she was receiving, traced her jawline with one fingertip and read about Rock Stars and Cocaine. Justina sniffed pointedly for Roddy Mix's benefit, and removed her elbow from the desk.

"What does the word 'leefful' mean?" said Miss Haugen and tugged discreetly at the waist of her pantyhose.

Justina sighed. She was on her own. Bonnie's class had gotten the word "droghte," but Miss Haugen changed it from class to class. Oh leefful, leefful, she hummed to herself. She tucked her leg under her, and leaned forward on her elbows. Across the aisle, Roddy Mix scrawled carelessly and drew a pair of goalposts in his margins.

Three seats back, Star folded *Rolling Stone,* and stuck it into her Chemistry book. Justina traced her jawline with one finger, and was annoyed that she couldn't feel any bone. She took after her father. Round eyes, round cheeks, and no jawline. Her father had also been bald before his twentieth birthday, as he often pointed out. Justina shuddered and sucked her cheeks in.

"Name, date, and hour at the top of your paper," said Miss Haugen crisply, "and pass them forward." She pouted into the face of her wristwatch. Lipstick still intact.

"Waffle," Justina wrote aimlessly across the bottom half of her paper, and passed it up.

"Roderick T. Mix," wrote Roddy Mix at the top of his paper, and reached back to collect the others. Star's was on the top of the pile, and he looked hard at the small spiky writing that floated with no regard for the blue lines.

He covered her paper with his own, straightened the pile neatly, and passed them to the front.

PART TWO

1

"I'm Justina Milford," said Justina Milford standing solidly on the porch. "I think we know each other."

"No," said Star, looking amused, "we don't. Not at all. But come in anyway." She held open the door, and Justina and Leslie stood limply in the kitchen. Well, thought Leslie, and how do you do? Justina swirled her eyes once around the room and threw her hip forward.

"Nice place you've got," she said much too loudly. "Very nice," she added, and Star walked languidly into the next room. Justina arched her eyebrows and followed Star's legs, which were wrapped in gold lamé tonight. They sat in three old serviceable chairs with battered mahogany arms and legs. Not at all the sort of furniture that you'd expect her to own, thought Leslie, nodding pleasantly. They looked almost as though they could be anyone's.

"Well," said Justina. "This is very nice."

"Very nice," said Leslie, and blushed.

"What do you want?" said Star, bringing one gold lamé knee onto her chair. The refrigerator started humming and Leslie jumped.

"Why, nothing," said Justina, sociably surprised. "It's just that—well, Les and I live right across the street, and I simply said to her, I said: 'Les, do you realize that we haven't even met that girl across the street?' Didn't I say that, Les?"

"Yes," said Leslie, looking at the floor. "That's what you said, Justina."

"That was very sociable of you," said Star politely. "But why?"

"Well," said Justina, beginning to look confused. "We thought it was a little odd that we hadn't, you see."

"Oh," said Star, and looked hard at Leslie, who smiled brightly. Star looked at the ceiling. "I didn't think you would," she said without looking down. "I certainly wouldn't have, were I you."

"It was Justina's idea," said Leslie quickly, and Justina frowned. Star laughed out loud then, and her face was all teeth.

"Lord," said Justina, flatly, but under her breath.

"I'm sorry," said Star, clearing her throat. She breathed in, and touched the tip of her nose. "It's just that you're so—funny."

"Actually," said Justina in her mother's voice, "we came to help you."

"To help me," echoed Star gravely.

"Yes. You see, Leslie and I see you every day—living right across the street, you know—and it seems to us that you aren't very happy."

Leslie felt appalled.

"Mmm," said Star, and for the first time she looked uneasy.

"And we know how hard it is to, you know, really get into the swing of things."

"Extremely hard," said Star sympathetically, and suddenly Leslie felt extremely foolish and wished Justina would shut up. The refrigerator stopped humming. "For they shall inherit the earth," thought Leslie irrelevantly.

"And so," continued Justina, crossing her legs and leaning forward, "here we are. We can help you, you see, like making sure that you don't get in with the wrong sort of crowd, and things like that. You know."

"Well," said Star, leaning forward confidentially. "I do have one question."

"Yes?" asked Justina, leaning forward even more, and just missing knocking heads with Star. "What is it?"

"How does one go about getting in with the wrong sort of crowd?"

"Oh," said Justina, sitting up and looking put off. "Well. You just do the wrong sort of things. You know. All too easy to do, too."

"Good," said Star gravely, "because the right sort of crowd looks just awfully dull." She stretched, arching her fingernails into claws. "I'd probably like the wrong sort of crowd much better."

Justina blinked. Leslie laughed out loud, and Star

47

stared at her curiously, mildly surprised. "Well," said Leslie awkwardly, "actually I don't think the wrong crowd is any better than the right one, you know. I mean, they're—well, they're both crowds—"

"You're right, Leslie," drawled Star, "of course." She stood up and the other two followed. "It was nice to meet you both," she said with a bright smile.

"Thanks for wanting to help." She smiled again.

They were suddenly on the porch.

"Maybe," said Leslie awkwardly, "maybe we can get together sometime."

"Oh sure," said Star, all teeth, "I can't imagine why not." The door closed gently, and Leslie stood with Justina in the wind. There were leaves hissing around their heads.

"Lord," said Justina flatly. "What a witch."

"For sure," agreed Leslie, and threw her face all smiles into the wind.

2

"See the fire sweepin' our very street today," sang Star on a Thursday night in November, as the first snow fell and tangled itself in her hair, *"Gimme, gimme shelter—"* She lifted her face to the dark sky. *"Shelter,"* she added thoughtfully.

Star's wet booted feet carried her automatically two blocks down and one over. They stepped firmly and sturdily, making no adjustments for the weather, while her eyes watched enchanted as snow fell lacily on the dry November city. People ran for taxis and umbrellas, and lights spattered like Christmas.

In the alley behind the Vagary Bar, forgotten piles of junk were sheet-covered pieces of furniture in a deserted mansion. Star skipped lightly up the three wooden steps and knocked with icy knuckles. The door swung open, and Meggie stood framed in slouch hat and pinstripes. Star giggled and walked in, stamping snow off her boots, wiping her nose on her sleeve, and shaking flakes from her hair.

"Meggie," she laughed with bright eyes, "you're Al Capone. My god, have you seen the snow? I just love—"

"Star-baby, we've been waiting. Look who's here. Rode in yesterday on a stolen Kawasaki—"

But Star had already seen Alec standing behind Meggie, and hurled herself at him before Meggie could step aside. "Alec!" she cried into his turtleneck, and struggled back to look at his face.

Alec was older than Star. He had masses of sparkling gold hair and an overbite that gave his face a pinched, ascetic look. His eyes were water colored and framed by a thick screen of lashes. The last time Star had seen Alec, he had been working for the Parks Department, and had been patrolling Como Park Conservatory wearing a badge. He was in the process of finding himself.

49

"Star, Star," he said, and a smile cracked a face that wasn't used to smiling.

"Mormons not good enough for you then, Alec," murmured Star. Alec hated loud voices.

"Mormons were a drag," he whispered back, and kissed the top of her head. "You're wet, Star."

"Snow," explained Star. "Alec, what are you going to do? I mean—you know. Just what?"

"Alec," said Nicky jovially, appearing from the walls and carrying a bottle with glasses, "is working for the *Prick*. I'm giving him a column, 'Travels with Charley,' that sort of crap. You know. Touch of the exotic."

"Could use a touch of something else," said Star, and sat down at the wicker table with London Bridge. She saw her face reflected in the window above Nicky's head and smiled as she always did when seeing herself unexpectedly. You're simply beautiful, she said to herself.

"Yes," whispered Alec, sitting down beside her, "you are. You're not supposed to know it, though, my conceited little Star. That's what the Mormons say."

"Mormons are a drag," she whispered back. She tossed her hair back and arched her throat, waiting for Alec to say something tight and amusing. Usually he did, because he enjoyed exposing affectation of any kind, especially when the affectation came deliberately and cheerfully from Star. But now he just looked, and said nothing.

"You're fey, Star," said Nicky, slopping amber liquid into glasses. It caught the light and settled. "Fey as they come. Here."

"Thank you," said Star, and watched fascinated as her arm reached out, snakelike, to lift the glass. Normally, she became nauseated at the taste of liquor, but at the Vagary Bar she neither felt, thought, nor tasted, and brandy flowed warmly in her like blood.

"Here's to Alec and the *Prick*," said Nicky, lifting his glass.

"Here's to Mormons on Kawasakis," said Alec, lifting his.

"Here's to coming back," said Star, tossing hers down. She kicked her boots off, and brought one knee up under her chin. "Is this London Bridge?" she mumbled.

"With a few hundred pieces missing, is all. I'm surprised that Connie didn't dump it."

"Connie wouldn't dump any of our stuff," said Star, lifting her head. "I was gone all summer, and Connie didn't touch my Rolling Stones—"

"I wouldn't either," bellowed Nicky, tossing another down.

"Because she knew I'd be back," explained Star, "and Meggie says no one leaves the Vagary Bar." She looked across the room, where Meggie was playing Mah-Jongg. Her eyes were hidden.

"See you two later," said Nicky, standing briskly. "My Pimm's chappie is back."

"Alec," said Star, as Nicky staggered from the room, "how can you possibly work for Nick's piece of crap?"

"Well, love," said Alec, sticking a piece of the Thames into a corner, "I don't mind working with crap, really, I mean, it's all the same, actually. What the hell, you

51

work with the Parks Department, or you work with crap, and who knows the difference? Who cares, anyway? Not me."

"Fine way to find yourself," Star remarked severely, and hunted for a piece of sky.

"Well, love, who can tell? I might find paradise at the *Prick*, you know."

"Not likely. He wants me to pose for him. My mother would love that."

"Not likely your mom is on the subscription list. She'd never see it."

Star shrugged and bent over the puzzle. Alec watched the back of her neck for a few minutes, and then started sifting through pieces himself. The London Bridge came to life on white wicker, and familiar faces drifted by to smile and help. Meggie, and Connie, and Nicky back from the bar. Happy happy, thought Star distinctly, and she was surprised to find that it was true.

"—definitely not suicidal," murmured Meggie to a heavy-eyed blonde, who was nodding into a Michelob.

"—faculty, which is simply declaring war on us," came Nicky's voice from near the window, where snow was gluing itself to the glass.

"—six cases and some cocktail onions," said Connie earnestly to a chubby boy in a raccoon coat.

Star looked at her face reflected in the window. Fey as they come, she thought with a grimace, and noticed that Alec was also staring into the window. "Alec I love you!" she said impulsively, and instantly regretted it.

"You what?" said Alec, sitting up and raising his eye-

52

lids delicately. Then he looked at her face, and laughed, and his face was suddenly younger than Star's. "Watch it, love," he said. "One of these times I might believe you, you know."

"Actually," Star whispered, "what I meant was—"

"I know what you meant. You meant that you love yourself, actually. I know you, Star." Alec settled back, and laughed again.

"Oh, for sure," said Star shakily. She laughed and tossed a piece of cloud at him.

"Star-baby," murmured Meggie, swaying over, all pinstripes. "Nine-forty-five, and hell outside."

"Oh lord," said Star, pulling on her boots and scarves. "Where's my— Alec, hand me that—no, the red one. Yes. Thanks. I've got to run now." She hugged Alec, and rushed to say good-bye to the rest.

Alec stood by the door as Star hesitated on the first step, poised like Venus before plunging into the storm. "Why the hurry?" he asked softly. "Why can't you stay?"

"Oh Alec," said Star, surprised. "My mother wouldn't know where to look." A wave of the hand, and she was lost in the swirling white.

"Wouldn't know where to look," echoed Alec thoughtfully, and shut the door on the Vagary Bar.

3

"Dull," said Justina, lying flat on Leslie's bed and sticking her feet into Peter Frampton's 23" × 35" smile. "Dull, dull, DULL. I hate winter."

"I like to ski," remarked Leslie. She was sitting cross-legged on the floor in front of her nine-inch Sony. Now she looked up, frowned, and pulled at the cuff of Justina's pants. "Don't put your feet on my poster, Just, you'll rip it."

Justina sighed elaborately and swung her feet over the side of the bed. Who's that you're watching?"

"Fred Astaire."

"Thrills. Les, what's the matter with you? How can you sit there? Why is everything so dull?" Justina stood up and paced dramatically to the window. I am cut out for better things, she told herself dramatically, and stared passionately out the window. It had snowed all night, and the sky was swollen and gray. Across the street, Star stood on her porch, looking through the mail and dragging her fingers through her hair.

"Justina, sit down," murmured Leslie.

"Can't," snapped Justina, but did anyway. She picked up the telephone, and unscrewed the mouthpiece. "Calling London," she said, yanking at a nest of wires. They came off in her hand, and she stuffed them back in. They sprang out. Justina scowled. She mashed the wires into the phone with the heel of her hand and clapped the mouthpiece over them.

"What are you doing, Justina?" murmured Leslie, without turning. "Don't mess with the phone."

"I'm not doing anything. That's the point. Listen to me, Les. We're not getting any younger, you know."

"Oh Just, knock off. I'm watching." Mrs. Olson came on to push her crystals, and Leslie rubbed her eyes and turned around. "What so you mean, not getting any younger? I'm not even seventeen till August!"

"Les, was Peter Frampton sitting in his room watching Fred Astaire on a nine-inch Sony when he was sixteen? No!" Justina slapped her knee. "And neither was Fred Astaire."

"Oh, Justina . . ."

"—mountain grown for better flavor," announced Mrs. Olson.

"If this keeps up," said Leslie, peering out at the sky, "they'll be opening at Snowcrest this weekend. Roddy Mix works in the Rental Shop, and he says they've been working the snow machines for weeks."

"I need new skis," said Justina as Fred sat down to sing with someone in yellow feathers.

"Mm," said Leslie. She and Justina sat passively as darkness filled the room slowly.

Fred and Feathers sang another round.

Justina swung her foot thoughtfully over the edge of her wing chair, and when Barbara Walters came on, she had to go.

"I do need new skis," Justina remarked at the door. Leslie nodded and leaned hard on the doorknob.

"Mm," she said. "Say, Just. You know what you were saying about dull?"

"Yes," said Justina, on the porch and stamping, even though it wasn't all that cold. Justina was a stamper. "What about it?" she asked.

"Well. Nothing. Except that you're right." Justina grinned because she liked being told she was right, and clattered home. Leslie stood against the doorknob while flakes filtered in and melted in the foyer. Across the street, one light blazed upstairs, and Leslie watched hypnotized.

"Leslie Ann!" her mother cried from the kitchen, "would you shut the door please? I can feel it in here, and the snow'll make marks on the tile."

Leslie shut the door. She looked at the vase of straw flowers sitting on the telephone table. In the living room, Katie and Keith played Battleship with their backs to a squawking TV set. In the kitchen, her mother was watching *The Dating Game* on the kitchen set, up to her elbows in Hamburger Helper.

Leslie went to her room. Peter smiled his benign 23″ × 35″ smile, and she made a face and lay on her back in the dark. Across the street, a light went out.

4

Star stood with hands jammed into the pockets of her jeans. She was staring hard at the nail-polish display in Michaelson's Corner Drugs, because Star took nail polish seriously. She leaned back against a stack of cold cream, and squinted so that the rack was a blur of pink. Too pink. She frowned and reached out to swivel the rack. Never shop in the suburbs, she warned herself solemnly, and smiled. She selected a jar of Poppy Red and held it lovingly, rubbing it lightly with her thumb. But Poppy Red was just a bit too bright, more suited to summer, actually. It was winter now.

The door opened, and bells jangled as Star felt a draft on the back of her neck. Still gripping Poppy Red, she looked sideways. Justina Milford. Star edged along the side of Cosmetics as Justina went to the counter.

"Paper in yet, Mrs. Barr?" she asked, stamping her feet lightly on the vinyl runner.

"Yes. School budget approved, new play at Valley Arts Guild, and Susanna Erickson's nephew killed in a car crash. The one at the U, you know. Frank. Frank Erickson."

"Too bad," said Justina cheerfully, picking up a paper.

She tucked it under her arm. "I need an eyebrow tweezer. Where are they?"

"What do you want to go plucking all your hair out for? You have lovely eyebrows. Some of these girls that come in—look like Martians or something."

"Well," Justina said, shifting defensively, "I need one anyway."

Mrs. Barr shook her head. "Over there, by the cold cream. Big stack."

Star turned her back delicately on the cold cream and fingered a jar of Wine. Justina storm-trooped her way down the aisle. She saw Star immediately. "Well! What are you doing downtown? Never seen you here before." She fingered the reindeer on her ski sweater, and looked at Star through rosily aggressive eyes.

"Well," said Star, "I had this sudden urge to buy myself nail polish, you see. I'm afraid I have quite a fetish for nail polish."

"Oh," said Justina blankly. Fetishes didn't come easily to her. "Well. I like this Coral Pink here."

"No," said Star decisively. "Not pink. I mean, if you're going to do something, do it right. Something dramatic."

Justina scanned the rack doubtfully. "Do you mean—like—red?"

"Not just any red. Look. Now what would you wear this with?" Star handed her the jar of Poppy.

"Well—I don't know. I don't think I would wear it. Myself."

"Summer," Star said, replacing the bottle, "T-shirts

58

and nightclubs. Here. What about this?" She flipped a bottle of Berry in the Woods at Justina.

"Well," said Justina, looking uncomfortable, "I'm not too—"

"November," said Star. She looked closer. "Just about right. Dark and kind of dull." Justina nodded uncertainly. "But—with just enough red, you know."

"Here's one," Justina offered, plucking at the rack with short, chapped fingers.

"Mmm. Not bad, but look closer. It's kind of gaudy, like in the Fifties. Gloria Swanson."

"Oh. Well. How about Color-Me-Dazzle?"

"That's mostly what Junior Highs buy when they're trying for sophisticated. You know."

"No," said Justina, irritated, "I don't. All I've ever worn is pinks."

"Mmm?" Star said, not really listening. Her eyes were bright, almost feverish, as she squinted dreamily at the rack. "Fall and winter," she said softly. "You can wear anything. Burgundies are good."

"Lord," said Justina flatly. She looked impressed. "I didn't know it was such a big thing." She looked at the rack through Star's eyes. Twenty-four round bulbs of shimmering color to dip your fingers in. She squinted like Star, and the bulbs melted into each other. Justina's eyes flew open. She snatched a bottle of Color-Me-Dazzle. "I'm getting this," she informed Star.

Star nodded politely.

"And this—" Justina flicked a Burgundy off the rack. Star smiled.

"And—" Justina scanned grimly. "This." She grabbed. "Good-bye," she added, and headed for the counter, where Mrs. Barr shook her head but rang up seven dollars anyway.

Star stood quietly in front of the rack. Finally she shook her head. Nothing she wanted. Suddenly the colors held no enchantment for her.

"Nothing today?" asked Mrs. Barr pleasantly, as Star came down the aisle.

"No," said Star, opening the door. Bells jangled. "Nothing today."

5

Leslie stood in the mirror and fingered her hair. It was seven-twenty-five, and Roddy Mix was coming over for the evening. Nervous. She stood back from the mirror and froze. Her sweater hung like a bag of Jell-O. "God!" she wailed, flying off to her room. Discarded sweaters lay in violent heaps on the floor, and Leslie pawed through them wildly. Six minutes later she heard a car and dragged herself into the living room, feeling hideous in a stiff new flannel shirt. The doorbell rang. Leslie felt like crying as she passed the hall mirror, but managed to open the door with a bright smile.

"Roddy!" she cried in an unlikely voice, and promptly

shuddered. It occurred to her that she sounded exactly like Justina, and she shuddered again. "Hello," she added valiantly as Roddy Mix walked into the living room.

"Sit down," she urged as he sat down. She breathed in once and sat down next to him. "Well—isn't this nice."

"Well," said Roddy Mix, smiling out of a navy-blue turtleneck. "It gets kind of monotonous, going out all the time."

"Oh! Yes," Leslie agreed. She smiled. "Monotonous."

"I mean, we're always just going. Going to a show, going to eat, going to a dance—whatever. We should be able to simply enjoy each other's company, don't you think?" This was true. This was what Roddy really felt, but looking at Leslie next to him, like an eager puppy wearing flannel, he was suddenly without hope. The bottom of his stomach felt thick and dragging, he wanted to be somewhere else, he wanted—well. He didn't know what he wanted. Not at all. He blinked and turned his face back to Leslie.

"—enjoy each other's company," she was saying, nodding earnestly. Conversation lagged. "Can I get you something to drink?" she blurted at last.

"Ginger ale," said Roddy Mix, and Leslie sprinted for the kitchen. Ten minutes to eight. It wouldn't look right for him to leave before ten o'clock. That meant— oh lord—that meant one hundred and forty minutes of couch sitting. She poured a bottle of Canada Dry slowly

61

into a glass, and wiped the counter. She emptied five trays of ice cubes into the bin, carefully refilled the trays, and selected four cubes for Roddy's glass. Back to the couch.

"Well," said Roddy Mix, "there you are. I was getting worried." Leslie laughed gaily—*Seventeen* said men appreciated a sense of humor. Roddy Mix, a man? She sat down. He had turned the TV set on, so *Laverne and Shirley* relieved them of the conversation. Leslie watched seriously. She touched shoulders with Roddy and chuckled when he did. At eight, he stood up to change channels. "Where's the—can't seem to find the—"

"Third dial from the top," said Leslie. "No—from the top. Other side." She stood up and reached for the dial. She slid against Roddy's arm and blushed. Lord. He'd think she was being coy or something. He smiled and put his arm around her waist. She felt her flannel shirt popping out of her waistband.

"Do you like *M*A*S*H*?" she asked loudly, and felt ridiculous.

"Yes," said Roddy Mix, and removed his arm. Back to the couch.

At the commercial, Leslie said, "This is really nice. I mean, instead of going out all the time," and smiled brightly.

"Mmm," said Roddy Mix, looking at his watch. The doorbell rang then, shrilly, sending them both to their feet. Leslie went to the door and prayed that it was Roddy's mother, come to take him home.

"Hello," said Star's voice from the front steps, "I hope I'm not—oh." She saw Roddy. "Oh look, you've got company. I'm sorry. I'll just—"

"No!" cried Leslie, flinging wide the door, "It's okay. Really. Come in."

"Well," said Star, looking uneasy, "I don't think it's that important—"

"Roddy," said Leslie, "you know Star, don't you?"

"Yes," muttered Roddy Mix, "I do." Silence. Star looked from Leslie to Roddy Mix and smiled slightly. She pushed some hair lightly off her face and smoothed the front of her Grateful Dead T-shirt.

"The thing is," she told them, "I need an extension cord. Can't vacuum under my bed without one, you see." She laughed a bit; the sound hung in the air. Spontaneity seemed out of place in Leslie's living room.

"Well," said Leslie, on her feet, and feeling the flannel shirt bunch around her waist like a collapsible life preserver. "I'll find one. Yes. Be just a minute."

"Thank you," Star called after her. She looked at Roddy Mix. It was a challenge, and he felt it. "Having a nice visit, I hope?" she asked.

"Yes," said Roddy Mix, and blinked.

"I suppose it's nice to stay in once in a while." Gravely.

"Uh—well yeah, it is. Umm—I guess so." Not handling this well. He pulled at his turtleneck.

"Why are you so nervous tonight?" asked Star, tracing the D on her shirt. Roddy stared. "You look nervous to me," she told him. She went on to the E. "Of course," she added, "I could be wrong."

It was her, of course, it was she who made him nervous, standing there like that, but he only blinked sleepily and said, "Well. I suppose it's Les. It's kind of hard sitting on someone's couch for hours. All that conversation and stuff."

"Conversation and stuff," Star echoed thoughtfully. "Why should you make such an effort? Doesn't sound particularly healthy."

"Well," said Roddy Mix doubtfully, thinking it over, "I don't know. You're probably right."

"Mmm," Star yawned, stretching. "It sounds like— so tired!—sounds like masochism to me. Wouldn't put myself through it if I were you." She smiled at him sleepily, but watching, always watching.

He said, "I guess everybody's got to go through some things. You know. That's living." Socrates in a navy-blue turtleneck. He expected her to shout at that one, or else to drawl out something sarcastic and cold. *That's living.* God. Was it actually he who had said that? But she did neither. She leaned forward, almost touching him, eyes dark and fierce, like little cups of dark chocolate.

"But you're wrong," she said. He drew back a little. "Yes. That's just what people say when they don't know why they're doing something—everybody's got to go through things, that's what they say. They shrug, they smile—silly! Muddling through things." She looked at him severely, chin up. "That's NOT living, Roddy Mix. I know living."

He blinked. He cleared his throat. He wasn't used

64

to people talking to him this way, but he knew what he had to say. "You know living?" he asked her thoughtfully. "Maybe you do. But I think your living isn't real, I think you don't live with the rest of us—" He gestured impatiently, finding no words he could use.

In the hallway, Leslie could be heard, shutting doors and dragging something along the floor behind her. The sounds were familiar. They brought Roddy Mix and Star abruptly back to Leslie's living room. On the TV set, the *M*A*S*H* theme was playing over the credits. And Leslie was hurrying into the room, wrapping extension cord around her wrist.

"—seems to be a bit frayed around here," she said with a frown. "Must've been Katie chewing on it again— think it's okay, though."

"Thank you," Star said, but Leslie thought she looked distracted. Going out the door into the winter air, Star hesitated, opened her mouth, then shut it.

"Yes?" Leslie prompted. Kindly. Maybe Justina was right, maybe this girl was a bit spacy.

On the bottom step Star turned back, and looked at Roddy Mix. "I think," she said clearly, thin arms shivering under the Grateful Dead, "I think my living is much more real than yours will ever be, ever." Then she was gone, trailing the extension cord.

"Well really," said Leslie, tucking her shirt in. Cheerfully. She'd spent the twenty minutes in the hall closet thinking of a supply of topical things to say on the couch. A whole hour's worth. "What was that supposed to mean?"

But Roddy Mix said nothing. He was smiling to himself. So Leslie shrugged and tucked one leg under the other. "What do you think about the crisis in the Middle East?" she asked him, and smiled brightly.

6

"—the chin, please. Tilt it please, just a bit—aaaah—good. Hold now—" Long-toothed and long-armed, Nicky flicked his wrist across a damp forehead, and fiddled with his lens. There was a blinding flash as he snapped the picture. "There now. Let's see. Let's have you—I know—turn around, and put your chin in your hand—that's it. No. Little bit higher—that's it."

At the end of the poorly lit studio, Star sat in shadows and lace. She turned around dreamily as Nicky's voice instructed her from far away. "Posing," she said to herself thoughtfully, "always posing."

"—up, up—hold. Very nice. Now I want to see your throat—look back. More. Little bit—there. Look up—"

"Actually quite narcissistic, of course," she said, feeling her throat throb.

FLASH.

"My mother would have a fit, you know," she said reflectively. "In fact, I feel foolish myself. Posing, indeed."

"—Could you possibly look wistful, love? Nothing heavy, you know, just a—not bad. Say, maybe—no, this is fine. Just fine. Now, hold there—"

"Posing," thought Star scornfully, "posing!" Her eyes stayed wistful.

FLASH.

FLASH.

FLASH.

7

"Calcium, plus two," said Leslie in her bedroom. Outside a watery winter sun was just disappearing. In front of Leslie, her doodle-covered Chemistry notebook lay open at a page marked "Common Ions and Their Charges."

"Hydroxide, negative one," she said, and sighed. She reached up to brush the hair off her forehead. It was amazing how fast hair grew.

"Ammonium, plus one," she said bleakly. Roddy Mix despised her, she just knew it. But, she said severely to herself, it certainly was amazing to find how much this bothered her.

"Phosphate, negative three," she said. I don't care, she added silently, I simply do not care. Out the window, she saw a light on across the street. It must be Star, she thought. The light went on at the same time every night. Star.

"Sulfate, negative two," she said thoughtfully.

It certainly was amazing how fast hair grew.

8

"So," said Justina, delicately stamping snow from her crepe soles. "So you'll come to our party then, Star?"

Star, wrapped in some foreign-looking woolen articles, looked at Justina and Leslie with something that was almost affection. They looked back at her with matching bland eyes, and matching bland ski jackets, and the wind ruffled calmly at the tops of their heads. Well, thought Star, one can't be alone all the time. After all. "Umm," she said out loud, pushing her wrists deeply into pants pockets, "Well, yes. I'll come."

"Good," said Justina abruptly, irritated to be finding herself staring at Star again. "You can come over early Friday night—umm, around eight—help us get ready. So much to do. I love it."

"Okay," said Star, up to her elbows in pockets. She looked down the street and stepped off the curb. Ice crunched under her heels. "G'bye," she said, grinning briefly at them as she headed for her house. On the opposite curb, she heard Justina shouting. She stopped.

"IF YOU'VE GOT BERMUDA ONION DIP,
BRING IT."

Star smiled and waved. Bermuda onion dip. She
walked up her front porch steps, tossed her boots into
the porch hammock, and hurried into the kitchen with
stinging toes. "Ma?" she called, opening the refrigerator. "Mama?" Something odd in a glass, with foil over
it. She grimaced and shoved the glass to the back. *War!
Children, it's jus' a shot away—*

"Star," said her mother, coming into the kitchen with
a stack of manila folders. "Hello, darling. Is there a
Xerox machine in this godforsaken town, by any
chance?"

"—shot away, shot away," hummed Star, dropping her
jacket on the table, and digging her thumbnail into the
end of a grapefruit. "There's one at the PO, but it's
twenty cents a page, and only works on weekends."

"Damn. Why did I ever want to live in a small town?"

"It's just a shot away, just a shot away," shrugged Star.
She sprinkled sugar carefully on the grapefruit, and sat
on her jacket. The cuffs were wet. "Guess what I did,
Ma?"

"Don't sit on the table, darling. What?"

"I told Justina Milford I'd come to her party this weekend."

"That's lovely. I'm glad— You're getting juice all
over your pants, Star, and it won't come out."

"Lovely?" Star considered this gravely. She could feel
the wet cuffs on the backs of her legs. "I wouldn't say
lovely, exactly. No. But it might be something of a kick."

69

"I meant it was lovely that you're getting involved. Making an effort to get along, you know. It's about time, I think."

"Oh." Star gently separated grapefruit sections, and frowned. "God. You think it's time?" She shifted thoughtfully off the soggy jacket cuffs.

"Well. I should think that—look darling, I've got to ride into the City and get these run off somewhere."

"Class plans?"

"Mmm. No class next Thursday, it's Thanksgiving. Means I'll have to throw the editing guidepoints in with something else—don't know what." She peered out the window, made a face, and struggled into a trenchcoat. "See you later, darling, there's eggplant in the freezer—"

Star waved lightly. She sat on the table and finished her grapefruit, arranging the seeds in a crooked V on her left knee. Then she jumped gently off the table, dumped the seeds and peelings, and walked slowly through the house. Twilight was falling, and the rooms were filled with blue haze. She passed herself in the mirror, and watched her face fascinated. After several minutes of this, she shook herself and laughed impatiently. "You are ridiculous," she told herself sharply, "just simply ridiculous."

Up the stairs to her slanted little room, and she switched her radio on maximum volume and lay flat on her bed. Some hypnotic reggae thumped through the room and pinned her to her mattress. She opened her eyes. Her eyelids were throbbing, and she noticed that the magazine faces were watching her curiously. Smiling at them graciously, she stood in the middle of her room and swayed. *Da-da-da-da-TWANG,* went the radio.

"Alec?" she called softly. *Da-da-da-twang.* "Alec," she repeated, her voice rising involuntarily. "I can feel you, Alec." Star put her hands over her ears, knotting her fingers in tangled curls. "Happy happy," she said softly.

The telephone rang, and Star jerked and froze. Then she strode into the hall and stood staring at the phone with burning eyes. "Hello," she said into the mouthpiece, and tossed her hair back. "Oh. Justina. What? No, I had quite forgotten—yes. Well. I can get—there isn't—what? Oh. Sure. Bermuda onion. Right, okay. No, sure, that's fine. I don't think—no. Thank you. All right. Good-bye, Justina, yes."

Slipping the phone back on the hook, Star looked at the open door to her room, and frowned. She crossed the hall quickly, and closed the door. Then she went downstairs, turning lamps on as she went. Wrapped safely in hundred-watt glow, she fell asleep on the couch and dreamed of Bermuda onion.

9

"Hi, come in," said Justina Milford on Friday night. She said it loudly, repeatedly, trying to be heard over the top-40 on the turntable. She stood graciously, shining with an excess of cheap gold jewelry, trying to remember names. Luckily, it didn't matter much since most of her guests, wearing that glassy party-hopping look, were more interested in meeting the keg.

Justina ran damp fingers through her hair and counted heads. There was Roddy Mix on the couch, with Leslie bending over him, looking intensely at an album jacket. Fleetwood Mac. And there was Lori Sellars, hair pulled off shining face, surrounded by her tight circle of admirers. Discussing the rhythm method. There were ten or twenty other heads too, half of whose names Justina could only guess at, and the other half who had been invited to fill gaps. Lonnie Welton, for instance, was an utter wimp but could open flip-top cans with his tongue and would perform if things got slow. Franny Barr never opened her mouth and turned quite pale if spoken to, but she had a delightful way of keeping coasters under the drinks and was good with a damp mop. Justina planned her parties well. At the moment, however, she was frowning and pulling at one of the Woolworth's chains around her neck.

"Les," she said urgently, sliding onto the couch, "have you seen Star?"

"I guess she hasn't come yet," said Leslie, looking up from the album jacket in some relief.

"You're looking great, Sal." Justina smiled to a myopic girl walking past holding one Frito. She turned back to Leslie. "So where is she?"

"Syl," said Leslie.

"What?" Justina pressed her hair flat behind her ears.

"Syl. That was Sylvia Hoyer with the Frito, not Sal. You said Sal."

"Oh. Where's Star?"

"I told you she hasn't come yet. I wouldn't worry about it though. She looks like the kind of person who's always late. You know."

"No," said Justina, looking up to grin at Lonnie Welton, "I don't know. I told her eight, and it's almost nine-thirty."

"You really can't listen to Led Zeppelin," came Lori Sellars' voice, "unless it's LOUD." Someone reached over to turn up the volume, and Justina stood up to mingle. There were things that had to be done. Katie and Keith, Leslie's charges, must be kept upstairs, and Lonnie Welton discouraged from lighting matches near the drapes. And the carpet. Already Justina could see a dark dampish spot under one of the end tables that showed signs of drying and remaining forever. She sighed and went to the kitchen for paper towels.

Later, emptying a bag of Screaming Yellow Zonkers! into a plastic bowl, she finally heard a knock. "Come in," she cried accusingly, flinging the door open.

"Oh Justina, I'm sorry," said Star, stepping breathlessly into the living room. "Really. I didn't realize it was this late. So sorry." She looked straight on at Justina and smiled. Justina smiled back, involuntarily. Star was wearing flannel pinstripes and lace. She felt eyes on her, always the eyes, but tonight for some reason she couldn't manage to laugh and find it a kick.

"Well," said Justina expansively, "you really haven't missed anything."

"I'm glad," said Star, eyes glinting. Over Justina's shoulder, Lori Sellars pressed forward, leading aggressively with shining face.

"Hello there," she said, sizing Star up with a quick onceover, a skill that she was depressingly proficient at. "I don't think we've met. I'm Lori."

"Star," said Star, and accepted a glass of warm beer. Steady, she told herself sternly. She allowed herself to be drawn into Lori's circle of shining heads, who were polite and watching. All eyes. But she knew how she must act, she knew how they expected her to be, she had spent an hour and a half walking around the block preparing herself. Gathering momentum. It had been very dark outside, and damp, otherwise she would have walked for hours. As it was, she wasn't quite sure that she was completely ready. Oh well. Too late. She sat abruptly on the arm of a chair and crossed her legs.

"Something to do with body temperature," said Lori,

"on certain days." Star pursed her mouth and nodded gravely.

On the couch, Justina had joined Leslie and Roddy Mix in the reading of Fleetwood Mac's liner notes. "Well," said Leslie presently, rubbing her eyes, "I told you she'd come late, Justina. Didn't I tell you she'd come late?"

"Yes," said Justina, not listening. She was watching Star, who seemed to be talking in an excessively glib sort of way to Lori's shining circle. Justina wondered what she could possibly be saying. In school, she said barely a word.

"Probably she wanted to make an entrance or something," continued Leslie.

"Well," said Justina, "she did that." The three of them sat blankly on the couch and watched. "Yes," Justina repeated, "she did that."

After a pause, Leslie looked sideways at Justina. "Well," she ventured, "she looks nice, tonight. Don't you think?"

"She does," said Roddy Mix dreamily, "she sure does."

Leslie bit the inside of her mouth, and looked at her wrists.

"Different," said Justina grudgingly. She was still annoyed with Star, but her party was going well. She had thought of everything, she was in control—she could afford to be generous. "Different," she repeated, and leaned complacently against the back of the couch. Voices and music. Not so loud that the neighbors would be calling, and not so quiet that there would be any suspicion of someone not having fun. And that was what mattered. Now, if only— Justina looked at Leslie sitting dully beside her, and sighed. She seemed to be staring at her wrists.

"Les," Justina began firmly.

"What?"

And sighing once again, "Nothing."

Wandering by with a Cheez-It, Sylvia Hoyer put one tennis-shoed foot on the coffee table in front of them. "Great party, Justina," she said. And squinting myopically, "So who's that in the stripes?"

"Thanks Sal," said Justina. "That's Star. She lives across the street."

"What's she trying to prove?" asked Syl. She wiped her hands on her Levi's, leaving golden flecks of Cheez dust down both thighs.

"Who knows?" said Roddy Mix, and smiled briefly. Leslie looked. Justina sighed and kicked at the coffee table.

In the circle, Star listened to the stream of conversation coming from her own mouth in some amazement. Listen to me! she thought. Me? "—in the bloodstream," she seemed to be saying, "but of course, I read that in *Cosmo*." Detachment. That was the key. Yes. But how much longer could she go on?

"Well, but I mean," Lori said, frowning with effort, "*Cosmo*'s *true*, isn't it? I mean, they know what's going on, don't they? I always thought."

"They pick up trends pretty well," said Star, waving

a limp, narrow hand. "But it's not journalism. And all those italics!" Listen to me, she thought, just listen. She imagined that she could see her face as if from across the room, tilted with interest, lashes half-closed against the light. Nicky would laugh. Alec would shout, he would take her by the shoulders and shake her. Star, Star, they would all say, oh, what are you trying to do?

Not much longer now. She must stop soon. Foolish. "Excuse me," she said, standing abruptly, interrupting Lori, who was explaining what IUD stood for. Where to go? There were people everywhere, mouths and teeth and eyes as far as she could see. They were draped on furniture, propped in doorways, and sprawled on the floor. Must step carefully. Finally she saw Justina, feet on the coffee table, and a bowl of popcorn between her knees.

"Hello," Star said, standing near the end of the couch, near Leslie. She propped a knee on the arm and looked down. "What's the matter, Justina? I've never seen you this quiet for so long."

"Oh—nothing," said Justina brightly. "Just—you know. It's wearing, being a good hostess."

"It goes inside, you know, but a doctor has to do it—"

"Are you having a good time?" Leslie asked Star.

"—so she said, she said, like, no one can tell anyway. You know? 'Cause it's inside, you can even forget all about it—"

"Well—" Star looked around the room, and spread her hands. "Yes. I guess I am. Is it—I'm just not used to so many people at one time. So hard to take them personally."

"Oh?" said Roddy Mix, and blushed.

"Yes," Star said, looking at him thoughtfully. "And I guess I'm not used to this kind of people, either."

"—STANDING there, you know, looking like an absolute fool, right there in the middle of Southdale—"

"Oh?" said Roddy Mix.

"But," said Star, spreading her hands, "what can I say? People are people, I suppose, wherever you find them."

"Lord," said Justina flatly, under her breath, and smiled up at Star.

"—said, 'Do you have this in magenta?' We all just screamed, and Kathy had to go out, she nearly wet her pants—"

"Oh yes," said Roddy Mix, "people are people. Oh yes."

"Except," said Star, to him, "when they're not."

"—god, I hate people like that. So we all thought we'd go on over to Brideman's—"

Somebody had turned the TV set on. It filled the room with harsh flickering blue light and Johnny Carson's brittle dry voice. Star blinked and thought of herself in pink hood on Harriet Island. She cleared her throat. "Nice party, Justina," she said.

"Not," Justina said, "one of my better ones."

"Actually," said Leslie, peering over, "it is, you know. The last one, everybody left at nine-thirty."

"Not everybody."

"Well. Lori stayed, but she will, you know. Sylvia Hoyer stayed till the Fritos gave out. About quarter to ten."

"Oh Les," snorted Justina irritably. She slid down on the couch until her chin hit her chest.

"The best party I ever went to," Roddy Mix volunteered, "was last year after the Spring Formal. Everybody went outside and threw hailstones in the parking lot. I was with Veronica Bersinger, and—"

"What's the best party you've ever been to?" Leslie asked Star.

"Oh," Star said. She rubbed her knee and smiled a curly smile. "Someday I'll take all of you to the best party I've ever been to."

"Really?" asked Roddy Mix.

"Really," said Star. They looked at each other. In Star's eyes Roddy Mix felt a challenge, but helplessly he looked away.

"Good night, everyone," Johnny Carson said. The band went into his theme song.

"Good night," Star said softly.

"Good night," Roddy Mix said, and blinked.

"Lord," Justina said flatly.

10

"Bless us O Lord and these thy gifts," intoned Leslie's father. It was Thanksgiving, a shining hazy day, and Leslie's family had just sat down to dinner. Leslie had invited Roddy Mix because his parents were in Monte Carlo, and he had arrived looking nervous.

"Which we are about to receive from Thy bounty, through Christ our Lord, Amen." Leslie peered over tightly clasped hands at Roddy Mix's crooked part, and breathed in. He looked up on Amen, and smiled briefly at her.

Mr. Armbruster took up the electric knife and raced it experimentally. The smell of electricity filled the air.

"Honestly, Ed," said Leslie's mother. "Why couldn't we have carved the turkey in the kitchen, like other people do?"

"The pilgrims did it at the table," he answered, whirring into the breast. Appreciative giggles from Leslie's brother and sister. Mrs. Armbruster frowned, and Katie promptly knocked her milk into her plate. Leslie looked apologetically at Roddy Mix, and scurried for a dish rag.

"We could be half done by now, if we'd carved in the kitchen," Mrs. Armbruster remarked.

"I want Seven-Up," Katie said.

"I'll throw up if those are sweet potatoes," Keith said.

"Asparagus?" Leslie asked Roddy Mix, and wished she was dead.

Forks clicked and water glasses were picked up and set down with gentle thuds. The electric knife lay on its back like a dead bird.

"So," said Mr. Armbruster. "So your parents are in— uh—Monte Carlo?"

"Yes," said Roddy Mix, and blinked.

"I'm going to throw up," Keith said. No one listened.

"When will they be back?" asked Mr. Armbruster, wiping his mouth.

"I said I'm going to throw up," Keith said, looking around the table.

"The thirtieth," said Roddy Mix.

"Just try it," said Mrs. Armbruster. "You just try throwing up and see what happens to you."

"Probably it's gas," said Keith. "Just gas."

"Salt," said Mr. Armbruster. "Good god, didn't you salt these potatoes?" Katie reached across Roddy Mix's plate to pass the salt, and left a trail across his Jell-O.

"Kate!" said Leslie. "Why don't you watch what you're doing, for godssake?"

"It's okay," said Roddy Mix. "Really. I don't mind."

More fork-filled silence, as dishes were grimly emptied and refilled. Leslie pressed her asparagus with the side of her fork and looked at Roddy Mix. His head was bent over a particularly restless piece of turkey, and a few golden strands veiled his eyes.

81

"Leslie's making eyes," announced Katie, pointing her fork. It slipped through slack fingers, and plummeted dramatically to the floor.

"For godssake, Kate," said Mr. Armbruster irritably. "If you drop one more thing, you're going to your room. Go get another fork."

"It's not dirty," said Katie, appearing from under the table with shining face, "I can still use it. See?"

Mr. Armbruster shrugged and forked a piece of dark meat onto Keith's plate. "I want Cap'n Crunch," Keith said loudly.

"You'll shut up and eat if you know what's good for you," said Mrs. Armbruster.

"I'm going to be sick," Keith said. He picked up his spoon and made craters in his sweet potatoes. No one said anything.

After dinner Leslie and Roddy Mix carried dishes out to the kitchen while Katie and Keith crawled under the table to play doghouse. Mr. Armbruster lovingly cleaned and wrapped the electric knife and hung it in the pantry. Mrs. Ambruster ran Ivory Snow into the sink and turned the TV on. "—Detroit buzz buzz on the twenty-eight-yard line buzz it's third and six—"

"Damn football," said Mrs. Armbruster jovially. "Goddamn football."

Roddy Mix and Leslie stood in the dining room and gazed intently at the table. It was cleared naked, except for a thin trail of salt running down one side. Leslie pressed her thumb into a crumb of roll, and picked it off.

"Well—" said Roddy Mix. Leslie ground the crumb into the side of her leg. "I think I should be off," said Roddy Mix.

"Oh," Leslie said. "Sure."

She dragged Roddy's winter jacket from the hall closet, and stood bleakly while he slipped it over his holiday clothes. On the porch steps, Roddy Mix looked quickly into the steaming house, leaned over, and kissed Leslie chastely on her hot mouth. I am insane, she thought, and smiled brightly. Roddy smiled, waved, and was suddenly roaring around the corner in his car.

In the house, Keith was gnawing the table leg. Leslie beamed at him, and he sank back as if she'd kicked him. In the kitchen, Detroit was punting and her father was drying dishes.

"What a lovely Thanksgiving," said Leslie, all eyes. "What a simply marvelous Thanksgiving."

She picked up the dish towel without being asked, and polished cups and plates earnestly. She felt their eyes on her back, smiled, and said not a word.

11

"So," Justina said to Star, as they filed into Brit Lit on Monday morning. "So how was your vacation?"

"I hate holidays," said Star, but she looked cheerful.

"What'd you do all weekend?" asked Justina, fingering her collar and wondering if anyone would notice that she was wearing new Levi's.

"Oh—" Star looked at the clock. Nine-eleven. "I went to the midnight movies in the City. Some documentary on the Rolling Stones. And Charlie Chaplin. You know. Great way to spend the night."

"Lord," said Justina, flatly but cheerfully.

"New pants?" Star asked, as she sank into her desk. Justina brightened considerably. Star tucked one leg under her, and watched idly as the rest of the class filed in. All faces and names belonging to mothers who ironed their jeans and fathers who spent their days at 3M Company and cleared their throats. Roddy Mix came in late, guiltily, and he smiled wispily at Star as he sat down. Happy happy, and Star thought suddenly and wistfully of Alec.

"Today," said Miss Haugen, clasping her hands benignly, "we start the *Morte d'Arthur* by Thomas Malory. This was the most influential piece of prose of the fifteenth century—"

Star watched smooth heads bending academically over notebooks. She saw Justina frown slightly over the spelling of "morte," and Roddy Mix start a new row of footballs in his margin.

"—is known about Malory, except that he was an English knight who wanted to preserve the spirit of medieval knighthood in his writing. The *Morte d'Arthur* was published in 1485—"

Star watched Justina struggle with "medieval," and Roddy Mix pen "1485" in the middle of one of his footballs. Out the window, sleet was sliding gently through the gray air. It would be snow by afternoon. Star shivered deliciously and wrapped her arms around her velour pullover.

"—you can see noble chivalry, courtesy, humanity, friendship, and virtue—"

Three seats up, Justina delicately penned something into the palm of her hand, and flashed it at Roddy Mix. He nodded, and his hair swung as he turned to face Star. Carol Neby, who sat between them, was absent and three empty desks yawned in a row.

"Justina wants you to eat lunch with us," he whispered. Star smiled.

"Of course," she said, graciously. Roddy Mix blinked and swung around. He nodded at Justina, who was smoothing denim over her hips and chewing the end of her Bic.

"—three parts. The Coming of Arthur, the Round Table, and the Search for the Holy Grail—"

The smell of sauerkraut wafted into the English Department and mixed with chalk dust and stale air. Soon, thought Star, I shall be sitting all in a row with Leslie, Justina, and Roddy Mix, and we will be eating sauerkraut and talking chalk dust. She expected the thought to depress her. It didn't.

"I," she said with eyes on the ceiling, "am a mystery to myself."

12

One block over, two blocks down, thought Star. Into the dark alley, where old piles of November leaves mixed with snow. Star blew on her hands and tapped the door gently with the toe of her boot.

"Star." It was Alec, flinging the door open, and spilling light into the alley. Star blinked. Alec was holding a pewter candlestick and cupping the flame gently. "You're just in time, love," he said softly.

"Time for what?" Star struggled out of her British fireman's jacket, and tucked red hands into the sides of her boots. "So cold," she murmured.

"Why," said Alec gravely, "Nicky's going to read his editorial."

"That's right," said Nicky, all teeth and brandishing a grubby *Prick*. Meggie, at a wrought-iron café table in the corner, sighed loudly and inspected her fingers.

"Really Nick," she said, "there's no need to put us all through this."

"Turn that thing off," he answered, pointing impatiently at the stereo.

"It's off," Meggie said, walking over and flipping it on. Derek and the Dominoes. "Was off, that is. Too bad."

Meggie was in ballet slippers over woollen socks, and a satin skirt. Her feet were tucked primly under her, and a glass stood untouched at her elbow. "So, get on with it, then," she said with a yawn.

"Well," said Nicky, suddenly self-conscious, "I don't know. It's probably not any good. It's just something that came to me one day on the freeway."

"Oh dear god," said Meggie, pulling a thread from her hem. She looked at Star across the room and smiled.

"So let's hear the damn thing," said Connie, rattling a jar of swizzle sticks.

Alec looked at Star and put his fist out. Star stared at his fist and felt her eyes go fuzzy.

"—seems to many of us that grading systems should be abandoned after high school. The prime motivation for college students should not be, as in high school, the almighty A. There is simply too much—"

Star put out her fist and poised it over her thigh. She and Alec thumped their fists three times on their legs, and then extended their hands. Star put out two fingers, and Alec showed his palm flatly.

"—where the whole idea of education is mandatory, there is a definite need for—"

"Scissors cuts paper," whispered Star triumphantly, her teeth catching the light.

"Two out of three," muttered Alec, bending his head so that gold strands of hair veiled his eyes. *Thump thump thump.*

"—kind of thing. Obviously, when a person works harder merely to get into the college of his choice—"

"Paper over stone," said Alec, with a satyrlike grin. Star shrugged.

"Excuse me, Nick darling," Meggie drawled loudly. "I really hate to interrupt—really I do, but would you hand me the champagne bottle please?"

"Honestly," frowned Nicky, stretching across the table for the bottle. "Here. Now would you let me finish?"

"Well, I'm sorry," said Meggie, not looking sorry in the least. "But would you have me listen to you sober?"

"Mmm," said Nicky. "Just a minute here—where was I? Futile climbing?"

"Oh, I think we covered that."

"Yeah . . . well, I can't seem to—oh. Here we go. Umm—yeah." Nicky rattled the *Prick* self-consciously. "The authorities seem to have an opinion of their own on the subject—"

Thump thump thump. Star and Alec looked down at their stiff fingers. "Ha!" mumbled Alec, "Paper covers stone again. You're covered, love."

"Best three out of five," said Star, frowning slightly. She wasn't fond of losing.

"—not only willing to give in to a hopeless bureaucracy that rebels against change of any sort—"

"Sorry, Star," grinned Alec, "but I seem to be all over you tonight. Scissors cuts paper, you know."

"Dumb game," said Star, laughing, "I mean it." She rubbed her knuckles.

"—and we can only conclude—"

"Can we really, Nick?" Meggie asked, standing up

88

noisily. "I wonder. I wonder if you can conclude any-thing at all, Nick. If you can, I wish you'd conclude this editorial, because if you say one more word about motivation, I think I shall vomit."

"So do you think you could shut up while I read this to the people who care about the state of the world?"

"Only if you do it quietly, Nick. I think that I for one would rather listen to Alec tell about the nighttime habits of Mormons." She shuffled across the room in worn Capezios, and made a face at Nicky as she went by. "Hello, Star-baby. What's news?"

"Not much. Alec beat me three out of five." Star frowned, and slid against the wall.

"Don't lean, honey, wall's not what it used to be." Meggie propped her knees against Alec's back and put her hands behind her head. "Sit still, Alec."

"You know what I did a couple of weeks ago?" Star asked solemnly. Meggie shook her head just as solemnly. "I went to a party," announced Star. "Yes. A lovely little high school party."

"Why?" asked Alec, turning around and bouncing Meggie's legs off his back.

"Oh," shrugged Star, "I don't know why, exactly. It's just that sometimes—I feel not quite normal. You know."

"No fun being normal."

"You should know," Meggie drawled.

"Well," said Star, "I didn't mean normal exactly. I meant that sometimes, when I feel alone, it helps to do something—normal."

"Flannel shirts," nodded Alec. "Class rings. Football on Friday."

"Curling irons," added Meggie. "Homecoming dances."

"Yeah," smiled Star. "Right. Well anyway, Leslie and Justina—they live across the street, you know—had this party. And I went, and I thought it would be simply ghastly, and it certainly wasn't the event of the year, but I'm beginning not to mind them so much. In fact—"

"Well," said Meggie, looking fleetingly at Alec, "you have to be careful with that kind of thing, Star-baby. Too much lightheaded socializing dulls the mind."

"Leslie and Justina, then?" smiled Alec, making it sound like a punchline.

"Yes," said Star, suddenly uneasy, "yes. But you're right, Meggie. I'll remember."

"I know you will, Star-baby," purred Meggie, rubbing the toes of her Capezios. "Because no one leaves the Vagary Bar."

"Not even me," said Alec lightly, and stood up. "Nine-forty-three, Star. And slippery out there."

Star said hasty good-byes, hugging Alec and Meggie, and wishing she never had to leave. It was so safe in the Vagary Bar. So safe and lovely. She sighed, but as she slipped through the alley, she felt cold air blasting against her face and breathed deeply. Fresh air made her eyes sparkle.

13

"But did he kiss you?" brayed Justina impatiently. It was the last day of November, and Leslie, Justina, and Star were walking the fourteen blocks uphill to school together. Sidewalks are built for two, so Leslie was mostly on the boulevard, but she didn't mind. She had often noticed that when there was a situation where one person had to walk on the boulevard, that person was usually her. It was one of the things she wondered about before dropping off to sleep at night sometimes, but it didn't really bother her.

"Oh Justina!" she cried, dodging a fire hydrant. "Do you have to make it sound so tacky?"

"So what's the big deal, Les?" Justina poked Star. "Don't you think she's making an awfully big deal about one goddamn kiss?"

"Well—" said Star, looking at Leslie's furious profile. She wrapped her scarf around her collar once more. "I don't know. It could have meant more to her, you know. We weren't there, after all."

"Yes," said Leslie eagerly, "exactly, Star. I don't know—I just have this feeling about me and Roddy. Like we're *meant* for each other."

"Oh lord, save me!" Justina brayed theatrically. "All

right, Les. So it's in the stars, so you're Juliet Clampett. Look. Let's just drop it, okay?"

"Capulet," Star said.

"Capulet what?"

"Juliet Capulet. You said Clampett, and they're the Beverly Hillbillies."

"Oh," Justina said blankly. She swung around to Leslie. "Did you finish your Chem problems?"

Leslie swung around a small tree with a wire cage wrapped around it. "Of course. They weren't hard, Just. All you had to do was balance the equations."

"Well then, what about number five? That one with the five-oh-two after the little dot? Do you multiply, or what?" Justina fingered the ski tags on her zipper.

"That just means it's a hybrid. Oxygen doesn't bond with the compound." Leslie glanced at Star, who was walking along between them and staring at the scuffed toes of her boots. Her eyelashes were tipped with frost. "Where are all those tags from, Just?" Leslie asked.

"Breckenridge last February. Look, Les. What about those things you put parentheses around?"

"Radicals. What about them?"

"Oh," Justina said. "Do you do the oxidation thing, then—Leslie, did Roddy Mix kiss you? Just say yes or no, and I'll shut up about the whole thing."

"Justina," said Leslie, and sighed. Actually, she felt quite important, and superior to Justina, which didn't happen very often. She liked it. She smiled. "Well," she said with another sigh, "yes. But it was very fast."

"How fast?" Justina said doubtfully.

"My parents were in the kitchen," Leslie explained apologetically.

Star looked up abruptly from her scuffed toes, and smiled dazzlingly at Leslie. *"Love, sister,"* she said, *"it's just a kiss away, it's just a kiss away . . ."*

Leslie looked at her and laughed delightedly. "Yes," she said. "Yes, exactly."

"Oh lord," said Justina flatly.

14

Star sat on a low bench outside the dressing room in Brett's department store. In front of her, Leslie twirled winter coats in front of a three-way mirror, and on her left, Leslie's sister Katie removed sales tags from a pile of discarded coats. On her right, the water fountain hummed. Star stretched her legs in front of her. She had agreed to help Leslie choose a winter coat mainly because she didn't want her to end up in a jacket like the old ski jacket that Leslie and Justina had picked out together. Now, in front of the stuffy fitting rooms, she wondered idly why she had cared.

"Well," remarked Leslie, twirling, "I still like the tweed better."

"Okay," said Star.

"Oh—I don't know—would you hand me that gray one, Star?"

"Give me the gray, Katie," said Star, standing up. Katie looked up with her fingers full of cardboard and her eyes shining.

"Stupid," she said cheerfully, "stupid stupid." Star dropped her arms and stared.

"Well," she said out loud, "just well." She pried the gray from underneath Katie and staggered into the fitting room, where Leslie was mopping sweat from the bridge of her nose. "Here," Star said, and dumped it.

"Thanks," said Leslie. She struggled into the gray. Her mouth tasted like tweed. "Oh dear," she said, looking into the three-way. "Oh, no. I look like one of the Flying Wallendas." She sighed and let the gray drop. "Why don't I just get a ski jacket?

"Because," said Star patiently, and looking at the water spots on the ceiling, "because just everyone gets a ski jacket. Simply everyone."

"Oh," said Leslie, "that's right. Where's Katie?"

"Out here, pulling the tags off those coats."

"Oh dear," said Leslie, poking her head out the curtain. "Oh really—Kate, cut that out. You want to get arrested, or what?"

"I want to go home," said Katie mournfully, coming in with fur balls in her blond hair.

"Well you can just wait until I find a coat. Go and get a drink."

Frowning, Katie dragged out of the fitting room with shoelaces streaming behind her.

94

"Should really tie her shoes," Star remarked, sticking her legs out in front of her.

"Mm," said Leslie from under a green pixie hood. "Mmm. How do you like it?"

"Well—" Star pressed her eyelids gently. "It's you, Leslie. Definitely."

"You think so?" Leslie twirled hopefully.

"Oh yes," said Star. *"Gimme, gimme,"* she sang softly, rubbing her knee.

"Good." Leslie bit her tongue and nodded. She laid the pixie hood gently on a shelf, and started to gather up hangers.

"Or I'm gonna fade away," said Star, putting the gray on its hanger.

Outside, with the pixie hood in a box and the sweat drying on Leslie's nose, they walked slowly. The cold December sun turned snow into strobes, and Katie complained that her eyes hurt.

"Good," said Leslie, pulling her along by one wrist. "Serves you right, Katie-brat."

"Stupid," said Katie cheerfully. "So stupid."

"You know," remarked Star, "a good sweater would keep you warmer than a coat."

"I suppose," Leslie said. "My mom wanted a coat, though." She shifted her box onto her hip and sighed. "Do you know, I just remembered that Lori Sellars has a coat exactly like this?"

Star nodded. *War! Children, it's just a shot away,* she thought.

"Well—" Leslie pulled the rambling Katie to a stop

95

in front of their house. "Thanks for helping, Star."

"Sure," smiled Star. *Shot away, shot away.*

"Although," Leslie added, "I'm going to look pretty cute walking anywhere with Lori Sellars." She shook her head. Star smiled, waved, and headed for home.

"Stupid stupid," Katie shrieked after her.

"Oh do shut up, why don't you?" scowled Leslie. She was thinking miserably of Lori Sellars' pixie hood. She pulled the door open.

"Stupid stupid," murmured Katie agreeably, and let the door slam behind her.

15

"Well," said Lori Sellars as Justina stood outside the Brit Lit door. "I don't know what you see in her. She's spacy."

"But a lot less dull than you, at least," said Justina airily. "Certainly none of your business anyway, who I want for a friend."

"Well," simpered Lori Sellars, smoothing her hair, "I'd watch out, if I were you, Justina. That sort of thing rubs off, you know. Spacy."

"Justina Milford," said Miss Haugen, "you're late."

Justina stomped to her seat, smiling savagely at Star on her way. Star looked alarmed. Justina sat down across from Roddy Mix. She had no idea why she was so angry.

"Today we're going to read a passage from Search for the Holy Grail," announced Miss Haugen. She beamed and nodded at Tim Comfort, who sat in the front row and never said a word.

" 'And thenne the kynge and al estates wente home unto Camelot,' " read Tim Comfort.

Justina crossed her ankles and frowned. Her knee-highs had fallen again. They sat like dead balloons in collapsed rings around her ankles. She reached under her desk and pulled. Static cling. Lord, thought Justina flatly.

" '—and soo after upon that to souper; and every knyght sette in his owne place as they were to fore-hand,' " droned Tim Comfort.

"Thank you, Tim," said Miss Haugen. "Continue please, Star." There was a pause as Star sat up and searched for the passage.

" 'Theen anone they herd crakynge and cryenge of thonder,' " she read aloud, clearly and precisely, in a voice that traveled smoothly from word to word.

Almost, thought Justina with a smile, as if she read this crap every day. She flicked her Bic from her hip pocket and wrote on her hand: Do you have a rubber band? She flashed her palm at Roddy Mix.

"No," he said from across the aisle. "Why?"

"My socks are falling," she confided. Roddy Mix blinked.

" '—and al they were alyghted of the grace of the Holy Ghoost,' " said Star, and turned the page.

Justina fingered an old piece of gum stuck to the bottom of her desk. She prodded it fastidiously, knowing it was her own gum fresh last Wednesday, and therefore not unsanitary. She poked a fingernail into it, leaving a half-moon crack. The clock said nine-eighteen. Justina pinched the lump of gum savagely.

" '—and eyther sawe other by theire semynge fayrer than ever they sawe afore,' " said Star, not stumbling once.

Roddy Mix drew suits of armor between the footballs in his margin. Justina counted the curls of the spiral on her notebook. Tim Comfort sat and said nothing. Carol Neby was absent.

" '—not for thenne there was no knyght myghte speke one word a grete whyle, and soo they loked every man on other, as they had ben domb,' " said Star, twirling a piece of hair around her thumb.

Da-da-da-da-DA, thought Justina and wondered what was for lunch. She looked hopefully at Roddy Mix.

"Chili and pronto pups," he whispered with a conspiratorial smile. Justina was thrilled.

"Thank you, Star," said Miss Haugen, licking her lips discreetly, and wishing she had a Chap Stick. Star stopped reading, and looked at Justina sitting solidly three seats up. Happy happy, she thought irrelevantly, and smiled at Miss Haugen.

Filing out the door with Star and Roddy Mix, and happy to have the *Morte d'Arthur* packed away and forgotten, Justina sniffed the air rapturously. "I smell chili," she announced.

98

"I smell pronto pups," said Roddy Mix.

"I smell the Holy Grail," said Star.

"Lord," said Justina affectionately, and smiled at the both of them.

16

"You out, or what?" said Roddy Mix to Leslie. It was a frozen day two weeks before Christmas, and the four of them were in Justina's living room playing canasta.

"Yes," said Leslie. She smiled at Roddy and started counting cards. "Seven hundred for basic."

"Four hundred," said Star, flipping over onto her stomach. She picked lazily at the sleeve of her Mott the Hoople T-shirt.

"Damn," said Justina, throwing down her hand. "Just when I was about to go out hidden."

Everyone counted cards busily, with Leslie making neat piles of hundreds, and Justina scowling. Star put her chin on the carpet and noticed a piece of Cap'n Crunch in front of her nose. "When do you get your Christmas tree, Leslie?"

"Christmas Eve," said Leslie. "Eighty, eighty-five, one thirty-five—Katie still thinks Santa brings it."

Roddy Mix added scores efficiently, and announced that Leslie needed one twenty to meld. "Oh," said Leslie, who rarely won canasta games. She made four piles of the cards, and shuffled neatly.

Justina frowned at her hand of black threes and no jokers. "This game sucks," she remarked.

"Oh really, Justina," said Leslie disapprovingly, eyes glued to her hand. "Go, Star," she added. Star drew a queen and discarded it. Leslie squealed.

"Honestly, Les," said Justina, annoyed. "How can you sit there and get excited about this? Lord." She kicked listlessly at the card stand. Cards splattered across the carpet. Leslie looked up, all accusing eyes.

"Don't say anything, Les," said Justina. "Just don't. I want to do something different. I'm not going to sit here the rest of my life, playing canasta."

"Honestly, Just," said Leslie. "Who's talking about the rest of your life? It's been an hour and a half."

"Crazy eights?" asked Roddy Mix, and blinked. Star smiled down at Mott the Hoople.

"I think I shall scream," Justina announced theatrically. She stood up and went to the window. Wind hissed gently in the darkness.

On her stomach, Star looked speculatively at Justina, standing like Juliet Clampett on the balcony. On the floor, Leslie looked up patiently, with eyes reflecting too many canasta-dulled evenings. And Roddy Mix looked at his feet, shoulders slumped forward and gold hair catching in his eyelashes.

"Well," said Star, flipping onto her back. Three heads jerked to look at her. Three pairs of eyes met hers:

100

one suspicious, one hopeful, and one vaguely amused. "Well," she repeated, getting deliberately to her feet. "If Roddy would drive us all into the city tonight, there is something I could show you." No one said anything, and Star swayed slightly on her feet. "Some people you could meet." She paused. "But only once, okay? Just this one time, do you understand?"

Justina was on her feet and into her ski jacket before Star finished talking. "I knew it," she said, grinning, "I knew it would be you. I just did."

Star felt uneasiness shoot through her, a quick but thorough flash of regret that sank to her feet. Leslie looked at her.

"Are you sure, Star?"

"Of course she's sure," Justina said heartily, handing jackets around, and looking more animated than she had in months.

Mistake. Oh, such a fool, Star thought, but too late now, here we go, boys and girls. What was she trying to prove, what? Roddy knew, look at those eyes, look how he holds the car door open for her, excessively polite. She sat in front with him. Where to go? She must go, though, now. Too late for anything else. Well! "Downtown," she said to Roddy Mix, softly. He said nothing, he changed lanes, he knew.

She could feel Alec, here, now, he was close. And oh, he was laughing at her, he shook his head back and forth, gold hair sliding across his forehead. Silly girl, look at you, you're losing control. Yes, control.

Pointing directions vaguely, Star noticed with a kind of detached fascination that her hand gleamed with sweat under the streetlights.

She couldn't stop now, not even if she wanted to. In her stomach, Star felt the dull sickness of disaster drawing near. Oh, just shit, she thought distinctly, mopping at her forehead with the back of her hand. Roddy Mix parked outside the yawning gap of alley, and looked carefully at Star. He said something softly, but Star heard nothing, because the eyes that looked at her were Alec's. Yes, she thought clearly, I shall die.

"Does anyone have a Lifesaver?" Justina asked from the backseat.

"I said," said Roddy Mix, looking uneasily away from Star's eyes, "I said, is this all right? If I park here?" Star nodded at last, and he switched off the ignition. In the car, there was silence. Spectacular.

"A piece of gum would be all right, too," boomed Justina, "as long as it's not Doublemint."

The door. Look at the door. Control. Star struggled to open it. Leslie and Justina tumbled out from the backseat. "Isn't this fun?" Justina giggled in a theatrical whisper. Leslie frowned at her. "Oh Les," said Justina, "don't tell me you're still mad about the card stand!"

"Do be quiet," Roddy Mix said to her, quite sharply for him, as they filed into the mouth of the alley. Justina stared.

"Well!" she said, and shut her mouth. Star went quickly to a short flight of steps, and the other three followed wordlessly, moving in slowly among the snow-covered mounds of rubbish. Star tapped the door gently with the toe of her boot. Wind whistled in the alley. Star breathed in. Mistake. Oh fool, such a fool—

"Harder," Roddy Mix suggested.

"Yeah," said Justina cheerfully, stamping a bit, "give it a crack."

Leslie said nothing, she was watching Star.

"No," Star said. She looked at her boot. And then she lifted her head with a jerk. "No," she repeated, "there's no one there."

Justina put her head to one side. "Do you mean—"

"She means," said Roddy Mix, "that there's nothing there."

Nothing? Not exactly true, Star thought. But she stepped back, back into Roddy Mix.

"Oh come on," boomed Justina, pushing forward and through the door. "Just what have we got here?"

Star knew what they had there, even before the four of them were standing in the middle of an empty room, surrounded by frozen dust, looking blankly at nothing. Not a sound, not a move. They had one very empty room, a room whose only inhabitant was a broken-down wicker chair standing in one corner.

Justina cleared her throat. "Don't," said Roddy Mix sharply. Star spun wildly around. Roddy was watching her curiously, eyes limply blue under gold lashes. Leslie stood like a lost dog, hands stuffed bleakly into her pockets, and a face that hadn't yet decided how to react.

I am insane, Star thought with a kind of wondering detachment, I am completely and utterly insane.

"I don't get it," Justina said. She was annoyed. She stamped her feet, she sighed.

"Let's go," said Roddy Mix. It was all Leslie needed. She nodded once and headed quietly out the door, down the steps. Justina opened her mouth, closed it, looked at the ceiling, and followed Leslie.

Mistake. She was a fool, a stranger. She felt a long shudder in her throat.

"Let's go," said Roddy Mix, briskly.

It was very quiet in the car going back that night.

PART THREE

1

On Christmas morning, Leslie Armbruster opened brightly wrapped packages containing a blow-dryer (even though her hair had gone beyond blow-drying), a clock radio, four gold necklaces, a silver Timex, and three pairs of hand-knit socks. She sat calmly surrounded by tissue paper and empty boxes, and watched the tree blink. It wasn't one of their better trees, as Mr. Armbruster was gloomily fond of pointing out, but it blinked nicely, and would be thrown out on the second of January anyway.

"Stupid stupid," Katie chanted happily. She moved her new dolls, all of them in jumpsuits and plastic boots, around the living room in Keith's Moonwalker.

"How many pairs of socks did Grandma knit, Leslie?" her mother asked, leaning forward in a flowered robe.

"There's no Thermos in this," Keith announced, tipping his new lunch box upside down.

"Three," Leslie said.

"Where's the Thermos?" said Mr. Armbruster. "We paid for a Thermos."

"Well it's not here," said Keith.

"I hope they're not acrylic," said Mrs. Armbruster.

"I hope you saved the sales slip," said Mr. Armbruster, "because we're taking it back if there's no Thermos. No use keeping it, without a Thermos."

"I think they're wool," Leslie said.

"Are we having breakfast, or what?" Katie asked, abandoning her dolls in a heap under the sofa.

"Maybe it fell out," suggested Keith, whipping up a storm of tissue paper. "Could've fallen out, you know. Maybe it fell out."

"On the other hand," Mrs. Armbruster said, "wool does have to be hand washed."

"Did you save the sales slip?" asked Mr. Armbruster. "I certainly hope you saved the sales slip."

"Is there bacon for breakfast?" Katie asked.

"Hey," said Keith, dropping the lunch box, "hey! What's my Moonwalker doing under the sofa, Kate? Didn't I tell you not to touch my stuff?"

"Stupid stupid." Katie beamed. "I didn't touch it."

"People lose thousands of dollars a year," said Mr. Armbruster, "because they simply don't save their sales slips."

"They're wool," Leslie said. "I can tell wool. They're wool."

"Bacon bacon," Katie chanted. "Bacon!" She yawned and rubbed her eyes.

"Kate busted my Moonwalker," announced Keith. "Can I break something of hers?"

"Cut it out, Keith," said Mrs. Armbruster. "You want to go to your room on Christmas morning?"

"She did," said Keith. "It's broken. See? There's supposed to be a wheel here."

"Didn't," said Katie. "You're stupid."

"The stores are counting on people not saving the slips," said Mr. Armbruster. "They make millions that way. Just millions."

"Leslie," Mrs. Armbruster said, standing up, all flowers, "why don't you put on some Christmas music while I get breakfast?"

"Bacon," said Katie, pulling her dolls out from under the sofa by their hair.

"The one from Texaco, you know," said Mrs. Armbruster in the kitchen, "with Perry Como and Bing Crosby."

Leslie flipped the stereo on. Bacon spattered in the kitchen. Keith hummed happily with his Moonwalker, and Katie crouched under the dining room table, playing doghouse.

Leslie looked through the front window at the house across the street. She didn't see lights. "Well," she said thoughtfully, pulling the shade down. "Well—"

"May your days be merry and bri-i-i-ight," sang Bing, "and may all your *Christ*mases be white."

2

" 'Shine, shine, shine!' " read Star from *Vogue.* " ' 'Tis the season to be DAZZLING! Let brilliant new accessories carry you into the New Year!' "

Star sat alone at a dark wood table in the public library, with her legs stretched underneath and shoulders hunched cozily into her sheepskin vest. There was nothing she liked better than to spend an afternoon in the library. Sometimes she spent hours in the foreign section with musty-smelling books open on her lap, rolling deliciously unfamiliar syllables over her tongue. Sometimes she sat in Adult Fiction and stared at the shelves of sturdy library bindings stretching to the dust-flecked ceiling. Quite often she did nothing at all.

" 'The bright New Reds will DAZZLE you,' " she read softly, and stopped. A long-armed, long-legged man stalked by with arms full of Classics, and Star looked up sharply. His mouth lifted cryptically and his eyes glinted lightly, and Star said, "Nicky!" into her vest. He sat down at the table behind her. She felt eyes on her back.

" 'Splashes of color will DAZZLE you,' " she read grimly. " 'The unexpected New Reds for your lips, body, and nails.' "

It couldn't possibly be Nicky.

" 'Dripping with rich, super-slick shine,' " she whispered. " 'It's quite the LOOK for this holiday season!' "

A chair scraped the floor behind her, and she felt the hair on her neck tingle as he passed her casually and disappeared into New Fiction. " 'Put your look together, dare to DO!' " Star gripped the edges of *Vogue* until they felt damp in her fingers.

He came toothily out from between the stacks, looking directly at Star and carrying shiny, cello-wrapped books. He appeared to be—oh lord—heading directly for her table. Nicky, she thought, looking hard at the New Reds, oh Nicky. But what can you do to me? He was almost upon her. Hello, then, she thought, and bowed her head.

"Excuse me, miss?" Star looked up sharply, blindly, wild thoughts blending visibly in her face. He looked slightly put off, and cleared his throat. "Excuse me, but I was wondering if you had a pen I could borrow for a few minutes?"

"A pen?" said Star, rolling the words delicately off her tongue. "A pen!" She felt like laughing, a pen. Steady, there. "No. I don't have a pen with me. No. Terribly sorry."

"How about a pencil?" He was looking oddly at her.

"No—" she answered, slightly strangled, and bent over *Vogue*. When she looked up, he was gone.

" 'Anybody can DAZZLE,' " she read methodically. " 'It's all in your head!' " She flipped pages, and watched models spin by, all of them in the New Reds.

Five o'clock and cloudy. Star stood up, stretched, and

pushed the heavy chair in neatly. "All in your head," she said with a laugh. She placed *Vogue* on the shelf. "All in your head!" she repeated, and walked out humming.

3

"—a watch, two gold necklaces, and an electric toothbrush," said Justina on the way to school the day after New Year's. "Also, a box of Fanny Farmer Turtles."

Leslie nodded.

"How's Roddy Mix?" asked Justina, wondering how many people would compliment her new silver metallic ski jacket. She patted the side pockets lovingly.

"Oh," said Leslie, "he's okay, I guess. Haven't seen him lately."

"Mmm," said Justina, sliding her jacket zipper down casually. Not liking the effect, she zipped it to her neck again. Her hair caught in the collar, and she impatiently shrugged it out.

"Haven't seen Star around either," Leslie remarked. She was in her green pixie hood, but since she'd had it before Christmas, she wasn't as thrilled as Justina. She looked down the street. "Don't see her walking. She'd better hurry."

"Well," said Justina, turning her collar up in back,

"I don't know about her. Ever since she hauled us off to that—place. Just don't know about her."

"Mmm," said Leslie, shivering. "Yeah. That was spooky."

"Naw," said Justina, smoothing the inside of her collar with a delicate finger, "I knew it was some kind of joke. Probably she thought she was being funny. She's odd, that one."

"Justina," Leslie said, "how can you say that? When we've become such friends. Really."

"Oh sure," said Justina, catching a glimpse of herself in the window of a parked car. She frowned. "Lord. What's the matter with this? Les, we couldn't be good friends with her. You know—sometimes when I look at her—well she's not all there."

"You're getting dramatic again, Justina. You always do that—but I like her. I really do."

"Only reason you like her," Justina said, "is because you don't know her." Leslie frowned slightly, but Justina was walking faster, so Leslie set her mouth and took longer steps. The school loomed ahead in the frigid air, and long yellow buses hovered outside the doors.

"There's Lori," Leslie remarked with little enthusiasm. Lori Sellars, cheeks aglow, thundered toward Justina. Bad weather became her.

"Lori!" Justina shrieked.

"Just!" Lori shrieked. She was flaunting a new hat-and-mitten set. "Justina, I simply adore your jacket! Is that ever crazy! Turn around."

"What, this dumb thing?" said Justina, twirling around

111

anyway. "This collar is driving me nuts, I hate it."

"It's terrific," Lori pronounced, and the three of them were swept into the building on a wave of student bodies, all of them in new quivering clothes like Justina's. Faces shone, and hair was battered into new shapes. Voices rose ecstatically. Justina breathed in. A new jacket, a new year, and she couldn't ask for more.

"Yes," said Leslie at her side, "but I wonder where Star is.

"Oh Les! Stop it with her, would you? What's the difference?" And she lifted her chin, determined to hang on to her headiness. But somehow, as she caught her reflection in the glass of the trophy case, her jacket didn't shine like it used to.

"Lord!" she thought flatly, and sighed.

4

"No," said Star, staring into her cup of coffee, "I don't think I'll come along tonight, Ma."

"Well, darling"—with her hand on the doorknob— "I know there isn't much to keep you entertained, but you didn't seem to mind that before. Are you sure? Who'll carry my briefcase?"

"Mmm," said Star to coffee-reflected eyes, "I know

it. Yes. But I just don't feel like going out tonight, if you don't mind."

"Well—" But she was already half out the door. "See you later, then. Be good—"

Clatter down frozen steps, the car leaping into gear, and Star was alone in the kitchen with coffee-colored eyes. Be good, she said gravely to herself, and burst out laughing. She cupped her coffee in one hand, and walked softly through her empty house. Star loved empty. "Empty," she said out loud. "But Meggie, I didn't mean to—"

The door knocked. Star frowned and tried to ignore it. She looked at herself unfocused in the mirror, and didn't breath. Silence. She let the breath out with a hiss, and heard the knock again. Damn, she thought distinctly, and went to the door.

"Hello," said Roddy Mix, and blinked.

"Oh." Star blinked too. They stood for a moment, and then it occurred to Star that she should fling wide the door and invite him in. "Won't you come in," she suggested doubtfully, hoping that he wouldn't.

"Thanks," he said, and filled the room completely. He stood limply, not knowing what to do with his hands. "Well, well," he said, and blinked.

"What do you want?" Star asked.

"Help," he said. Star's eyebrows lifted delicately. "Chaucer," he added, "I mean *Morte d'Arthur.* You know."

"I'm kind of busy. Yes. Busy."

"Oh please," said Roddy Mix politely, "won't take

113

long. Just a few things—" He hesitated for a moment, then sat solidly on the couch. Star stood with stiff knees. Roddy Mix looked up. Star sat reluctantly beside him. "Well—" he said, opening his folder and sifting through papers. "Here we are—umm—yeah."

Star took the textbook from Roddy's cold hands and opened it. There were footballs drawn up and down the margins. " 'We myght not see the Holy Grayle, it was soo precyously covered,' " she read softly.

"Star," Roddy Mix said, without blinking.

Star looked up. Alec. Ridiculous. She went back to the book. " 'I shall laboure in the quest of the Sancgreal,' " she said clearly.

"Star."

Reluctantly, she looked up.

"I didn't come to talk about the Holy Grail."

"You didn't," Star said, her eyes moving restlessly. Be good, be good.

"What happened that night in the alley?"

"Hmm," said Star. "I don't know. I made a mistake. Quite a large mistake."

"Yes," Roddy said, his eyes Alec's, "you did. What was it?"

"Oh—" Star jumped off the couch. She faced Roddy Mix, eyes wide, and hands moving aimlessly up and down her thighs. "Do you want something to drink?"

"Why do you look at me like you do?"

"Coffee? Seven-Up?"

He followed her to the kitchen. She opened the refrigerator and ducked inside. He put a hot hand on her wrist and she jumped aside. The door slammed shut. She swung around, air flashing past her open mouth. "Look. Would you please leave me alone? I don't have to answer any questions for you. Now cut it out."

Silence.

"Well," said Roddy Mix and blinked. He suddenly didn't look anything at all like Alec. Star was relieved.

"Now," she said, all smiles, "let's get back to the Holy Grail."

"Yeah," sighed Roddy Mix, "okay. Back to the Holy Grail."

5

"What was the greatest piece of prose in the fifteenth century?" asked Miss Haugen distinctly. She rustled her notebook crisply.

"Mord Author," wrote Justina Milford promptly, and felt pleased with herself. She placed her pencil carefully at the top of her desk and folded her arms across her chest.

"When was the *Morte d'Arthur* published?" Miss Haugen slipped her tongue behind her front teeth. She'd had bacon for breakfast, and bits had stayed between her teeth all morning.

"Eighteen forty-five," wrote Justina blithely, and patted the hair above her collar. She had tried highlighting it the night before, and had done something drastically wrong. There were some dreadful yellow strands mixed in with some brassy red ones, and also a peculiar smell that had refused to wash out, but Justina didn't mind. Actually, she thought reflectively, it made her face look kind of interesting. Yes. She patted her head again.

"Name three of Malory's favorite themes," said Miss Haugen, easing her tongue discreetly into the space between her front teeth. Should have had cinnamon toast instead.

"Chivalry," wrote Justina steadily, and paused. Across the aisle, Roddy Mix looked preoccupied. Justina raised her eyebrows. Three seats back, Star rustled quietly through the *Twin Cities Reader*, and hummed listlessly. And always the same old tune, thought Justina annoyed, doesn't she know another? "Humanity," she scrawled scornfully. "Virtue."

"Name the three parts of the *Morte d'Arthur*," said Miss Haugen, slipping her red Bic into the corner of her mouth and probing gently at her biscuspid. Only coffee and toast after this, for sure. Usually she didn't have bacon anyway. She really wasn't fond of it particularly, and it took so long to make in the morning. You had to haul out the frying pan, and then stand over it so that it wouldn't burn, or spatter all over the stove. Big mess. She couldn't imagine why she'd bothered this morning.

"Coming of Author," wrote Justina. Roddy Mix sighed across the aisle, and let his pen trickle an answer.

116

Three seats back, Star bent darkly over her paper and momentarily ceased humming. "The table," wrote Justina doubtfully, and laid her pencil down.

Outside the window, sun blazed fluorescently on the snow. Justina blinked. Star looked up from her paper. Her eyes met Justina's briefly, and Justina thought distinctly that there was something she should note about the look in Star's eyes, but being Justina, she didn't. "Search for the Holy Grail," she wrote calmly.

"Name, date, and hour," said Miss Haugen. Justina dotted her i's gracefully, and handed her paper up.

"Damn tests," she remarked pleasantly to Roddy Mix in the hall. "Goddamn tests. And wasn't Haugen a witch this morning."

"Mmm," said Roddy Mix, and blinked.

"It was almost," Justina continued with a yawn, "almost as though she had a piece of bacon in her teeth, or something."

6

Happy happy, thought Star, aimlessly stalking city streets on a subzero Thursday night. Happy happy.

"Coward," she told herself accusingly, hopping gently on the curb in front of a DONT WALK. "You could look at least. You really should, you know."

The light changed, and Star found herself flowing across the street in a body of nocturnal sidewalk-stalkers like herself. The woman next to her had a tight little mouth with lines traveling from the corners of her nose to her lower lip. Not unlike Connie's, thought Star to herself, and turned abruptly into Donaldson's Department Store.

"However," she said, "I do have other things to do." She did. Her mother had pushed a list into her heavily mittened hand after Star had plonked the briefcase on the table. Eighteen pairs of eyes had risen over eighteen spiral notebooks, and watched her. She was becoming sick of people watching her. Almost. Not quite. "—if they have the paperback," her mother had said, "but most likely they won't. Also, would you get half a dozen date bars in Donaldson's bakery? Sixty-nine cents. Here. I've only got a twenty. Don't lose the change. Then across the street, there's that natural food store, and I need half a pound of carob and some vitamin E. Ask if the special is still on, won't you? The paper said until the twenty-third, but of course you can never—you won't forget anything?"

"Of course not," Star said out loud, pushing in front of a glass case. Inside there were silk scarves, arranged in a heavily contrived heap to suggest a South Seas summer. Star sighed, and walked on.

Now she was on the escalator, staring at the ridged steps, and heading for Better Paperbacks. *"Oh a storm . . ."* she sang tonelessly, and calmly watched the receding first floor. Off the escalator. "But you know," she remarked to *The Joy of Sex*, prominently displayed to slam faces coming off the escalator, "I really don't have the time tonight."

They didn't have it in paperback. Star stopped in the Third Floor Lounge and stood stoically in front of a mirror. Under the Lounge lighting, she saw a troubled face under a dark mess of hair. She was surprised. "I look definitely unstable," she said, and giggled at the thought. Unstable. The face in the mirror smiled too, and the mouth widened over its neck. Star ran her fingers through her hair, dragging it off her cheeks and behind her ears. Bones stuck out like piano keys. Star frowned, and watched fascinated as the dark brows drew together in the mirror.

"You do have fun, don't you?" remarked an amused voice from the next mirror, and Star felt foolish. She looked beyond her face and saw a tall calm face behind hers. "Don't feel foolish," the tall calm voice said. "It's great that you enjoy your face. I wish I could."

Star examined the next mirror. It didn't hold a particularly outstanding face. It was in fact quite plain. It was also familiar. Star sighed. She was tired of seeing the Vagary Bar in every face she encountered. "Well," she said, because the silence was becoming thick, "I don't really have all that much fun."

"Sure you do. It shows. Not that I blame you, you know. You're quite beautiful."

"Well," said Star, feeling ridiculous. "thank you. You're—umm—"

"I'm plain. I know it. Alas," she sighed, patting tall

119

calm cheeks, "we can't all be stunning. There have to be people like me, to make people like you look good. Don't you think?"

"Hmm," said Star, trying not to laugh, "I suppose so. Do I know you, though?"

"No," said the tall calm face.

"Oh." Star stepped away from the mirror. "I think I've got to go. Got things to do."

"Oh? Like what?"

"Well," Star answered, "carob and so on. Vitamin E, if the special is still on."

"You'd best be running, baby."

"Date bars," said Star, staring. "Half a dozen."

"I'm sure you have to do lots of things." The tall calm face stepped away from the mirror and collected her purse from the sink. "Just loads of things. Make sure you don't forget anything. Lots of stops to make tonight." She smiled briefly and went out.

Star heard cash registers jangling. *"Gimme,"* she sang tonelessly into the mirror. *"Gimme shelter . . ."* Her eyes were pools of coffee. She felt suddenly revolted, and turned swiftly.

On the way back to the University, with the white bakery bag of date bars cradled gently in one elbow, Star passed the Vagary Bar and her feet stopped on the frozen sidewalk. Cold. It looked nothing like the shadowy, comforting room Star thought she knew so well. She hesitated. It was simply a matter of turning

120

the corner and slipping into the dark alley. And then everything would be fine.

Her feet didn't move.

A blast of January wind shot down the sidewalk and she let herself be blown past the corner, and past the dark alley. "Unstable," she mouthed to herself thoughtfully. "Oh, very definitely unstable."

7

Justina sat solidly at the breakfast table, reading the back of the cereal box and listening hopefully to WCCO for school closings. Her shoulders hunched solidly inside green flannel.

"—will be closed today. Albert Lea, public and parochial; Alexandria School District 109; Anoka; Austin; Bemidji, public and parochial; Blue Earth; Byron—"

Justina was eating Kaboom with crushed pineapple, and drinking last night's Diet Pepsi. She had beaten Leslie at canasta last night, and gone through almost two six-packs. Justina shook her head reminiscently. It was the last hand that had done Leslie in. Four red threes, and a natural in queens. Leslie had only managed to put down a pair of sixes with a deuce, and by then it was too late.

"—Duluth schools; Ely; Excelsior; Fairmont; Faribault; Fergus Falls; Forest Lake, no Sunshine Nursery School—"

Funny thing was, Leslie had actually dealt her the red threes. Really. She'd almost fainted when she saw them in her hand like that. All in a row. Great game, canasta. And so easy to cheat if you happened to be keeping score! Justina had added countless extra hundreds to her score, and Leslie had never caught on. Of course, thought Justina, adding more milk to her Kaboom, some people just *don't* catch on. Ever.

"—Genesee; Genoa City; Gillett; Grantsburg district 24; Green Lake; Hibbing—"

And some people do. Justina frowned and thought of Star. Definitely something spooky about the girl. No one could ever accuse Justina of being an expert on human nature, and she barely knew what the phrase meant, but in a roughly blind sort of way, Justina picked up feelings about people.

"Giddy," she said thoughtfully. The Kaboom was turning her milk purple. "Not quite real," she added. She swallowed her crushed pineapple in one gulp. "That's it. Not real—a dreamer. A loser." Justina burped delicately, wiped her mouth, and put Star out of her mind. Thinking made her ears ring.

"—public and parochial; Hokah; International Falls; La Crescent, and no morning kindergarten—"

Damn. Justina, sighing, switched the radio off. You'd think she'd get a break once in a while, wouldn't you? She stretched, put the Diet Pepsi empty on the sink, and headed for her room to get dressed. Turtleneck ski sweater today; it was thirteen below.

Lord. Justina shook her head and grinned. Four red threes and a natural in queens!

8

"Oh Katie, do shut up," said Leslie, her face all scowls.

"Is that how they tell you to manage in that class?" Star asked, eyeing Katie from under frost-tipped eyelashes. Katie was strutting importantly to school for Leslie's Family Living class.

"But only," Leslie had pointed out, "because you get ten extra credit points for bringing in a kid."

"Why?" Star asked, looking curiously at Katie beaming along the sidewalk with a construction paper circle pinned to her parka: KATIE ARMBRUSTER AGE 5.

"Well," said Leslie, yanking her sister along the crosswalk, "we're supposed to—"

"Ow! Ow!" cried Katie. "Throw up, throw up!"

"She's been listening to Keith too much," Leslie explained calmly. "But the reason for this is, we're supposed to apply all this crap we've been doing in Family Living. So all these brats are coming in, and we're supposed to entertain them or something."

"Mmm," said Star. Katie set her head back on fur-lined shoulders, and fixed her eyes on Star. Star shifted uneasily. "Where's Justina?" she asked Leslie.

"Taking the day off. Buying shoes. Big sale at the Mall, you know."

"Shoes," Star said blankly.

"Shoes, shoes!" bellowed Katie. "Stupid stupid shoes."

"Knock it off, Kate," said Leslie through closed teeth. They stopped at a curb, and Katie hopped gently from curb to gutter, with her eyes on Star's face. "Crepe soles," added Leslie suddenly. "Yes. That's what she's looking for, Justina."

"I'm walking with *her*," Katie announced, appearing swiftly at Star's side, a small bundle of blue parka. Star jumped. Katie held her wrist out obligingly.

"All right, Katie-brat," said Leslie, "you walk with Star, then. Stay on the sidewalk."

"Stupid sidewalk," chanted Katie. "Stupid sidewalk shoes."

"Probably suede," Leslie said, tossing her scarf over her shoulder. "Justina likes suede."

Star nodded and held Katie's wrist like a slice of raw fish. It was limp. It occurred to Star that she ought to look down and make sure that Katie was following the wrist. She decided not to bother. "—for the Leap Year Dance, you know," Leslie was saying blithely. "I suppose I'll need new shoes too. That's a while off though." She sighed. "January is a pain."

Star looked at the gray sky. "Oh, I don't know. January is safe."

124

"January is a killer." They entered the school gates. Buses roared, and shrill groups of sophomores stood around stamping the cold with their crepe soles. Leslie was relieved to notice other Family Living members dragging their own five-year-olds. "Come on, Katie-brat," she said, "this way. And behave yourself, please. I don't— 'Bye Star, see you later—I don't want to be embarrassed, do you hear?"

"Stupid," glared Katie, stuffing a mitten in her mouth. "Stupid you!"

"Good-bye," Star said softly. Softly because she was through the doors and some way down the hall, and it didn't look good to talk to herself in school. Or anywhere. "Good-bye," she said softer yet. "Good-bye, stupid."

9

"Well, said Justina, pacing the Shoe Department importantly in five-inch heels. "She's getting spacier, you know what I mean?"

"I told you," Lori simpered, crossing her legs. "Didn't I tell you? I can tell that sort of thing, Justina. I'm perceptive that way."

"Hmm," said Justina, teetering discreetly in front of the mirror. She pulled at the cuffs of her pants. "I don't think these are quite . . ." She staggered into a chair.

"I never liked her," Lori continued, narrowing her eyes conspiratorially. "You can't get at her. Know what I mean?"

"Hmm," said Justina, heavy fingers pulling at sandal straps. "Good lord, how are you supposed to get out of these things? There. Well you know, there was a time when I thought—would you—thanks. There was a time when I thought there was hope for her. I mean, I really liked her for a while."

Lori nodded. She rubbed her feet raptly on the carpet and leaned forward. Sparks flew. "She even looks odd, you know. All that funny— Well. I wouldn't be surprised if she was on welfare, even."

Justina scuffed into a pair of maroon loafers, and arched her ankles experimentally. Her feet looked like pickled beets. She made a face and stood up. "All I know," she informed Lori, who was at the moment eyeing a pair of boys coming off the elevator, "all I know is, there was hope for her, and she blew it."

Lori turned back reluctantly as the boys headed for Stereo, and laid her arm along the back of her chair. "Those are cool, Justy. I like them."

"Well—" Justina squinted into the mirror. "The thing is, I have to wear them to the Leap Year Dance. I don't know if I have anything maroon to match."

"Who's taking you?" Lori asked, perking up noticeably.

Justina backed away from the mirror. "Well. Don't tell Leslie for godssake, but I think—I'm not sure, you

126

know—but I think Roddy Mix might ask me."

"Really?" Lori sat up in her chair. "Well—Justy! That's marvelous, but how do you know he's through with Leslie?"

"Oh—" Justina waved an expert hand airily. "Geez. I just know. You'll see."

Lori was impressed. She volunteered to carry Justina's maroons on the way home.

"Gee, thanks," said Justina, handing her packages over. Outside, the sun swept brilliantly across the parking lot.

"Well," Lori simpered, "what are friends for, after all, Justy?"

Justina, who had no idea, smiled into the sun and said nothing.

10

"The point is," pointed out Meggie, her voice like baby powder, "you don't bring visitors around here."

"The point is," Star muttered, "you weren't here. Nothing was here. It was— They thought I was crazy . . . like I'd made the whole thing up." She looked up, eyes blazing. "How could you do that to me?"

"Oh, baby—" Meggie was on her knees in front of

Star, her batik dirndl sagging around her like colored sand. "Don't say that."

"Well it's true."

"We're here now," Alec said from the corner, mostly in shadows. Star could see only his thumbs hooked in the pockets of satin pants.

"Yes," Meggie added, "and we won't leave you again. Promise."

Star tried hard to glare, but the familiar Vagary blood was running through her, making her sluggish. So tired. Meggie, watching through anxious eyes, started to smile, and reached out a long hand. She smoothed Star's hair and wiped her burning forehead.

"Come on," she whispered. "Smile for us, Star-baby."

Muddy Waters sang heavily on the turntable, and Star struggled to stay awake. "No," she said, "I won't. You know Meggie, I just might leave the whole lot of you. Yes! Someday—and how do I know I can trust you? I should just leave. And I might."

Meggie's mouth stiffened into a fishhook-shaped curve. Alec laughed softly from the corner. "Oh love," he chuckled, "I don't think so. I mean—look at me. Where have I gotten, running away from the Bar? It's a big pain out there—Mormons and so on. You know that." He leaned across and kissed Star on the forehead. "You know where you belong."

Star tried hard to remain sulky.

"Don't be like that, baby," Meggie whispered, triumph in her eyes. "Please smile for us."

"Oh Meggie!" Star burst out laughing. "You're so—

well, I'll get you someday. You'll see. You think you're so damn clever."

"You'll show us, won't you, baby?" said Meggie benignly. Star, still laughing, tried to nod gravely. Meggie shook her head. "You're so pretty, you know that?"

"Yes!" Alec cried. "Yes, she knows it, she knows it." He smiled at Star, who convulsed again.

"Oh do calm down," Meggie said briskly. "Really. We've only got till ten o'clock to celebrate Star's return, you know."

Happy happy, thought Star, and got to her feet.

11

"It's him at the door," Keith announced to Leslie, swinging around the hallway with Cap'n Crunch under one arm.

"I know it, Keith-brat," said Leslie, and clenched her fists in front of her bedroom mirror. "Why don't you answer the door, please?" Keith flew downstairs—"I'll get it, I'll get it" at the top of his lungs, trailing cereal on the steps. Leslie bit her lip and looked balefully at her T-shirt: Here today, gone to Maui. Justina had brought it back from Hawaii in ninth grade. It wasn't a bad T-shirt. Then—oh god—then she saw that it was dark and wet under the arms, and ripped it over her head, mortified. Oh god. She looked wildly around her room.

"Come down, Les!" Keith shrieked from the bottom of the steps. "I let him in already!"

Help, thought Leslie distinctly, and pushed her face through a turtleneck. Her hair went flat. Down the stairs.

"Hello," she said, smiling brightly. "Hello, Roddy."

"You look funny, Les," Keith said, picking his teeth. "Is it your stomach again?"

"Hi, Leslie," said Roddy Mix, hair shining serenely.

"Go upstairs," Leslie hissed to Keith, and kicked him gently in the kneecap. He went.

"Well—" said Leslie, leading Roddy Mix to the sofa. The TV spat angrily.

"Yes?"

"—from the pain and itch of swollen hemorrhoidal tissue?" asked the TV.

"Nothing," said Leslie, and wished she were dead.

"—prompt, temporary relief or your money back—"

It occurred to Leslie that she really wasn't all that fond of Roddy Mix. Well. There they sat, two faceless blobs in a living room, and neither of them with anything to say. Dull! thought Leslie, and turned to smile brightly at Roddy.

"—tonight's guests include Phyllis Diller, Dr. Felix Pepin, and the Flying Wallendas—"

If it wasn't for the embarrassment of not having a boyfriend, she'd drop him in a minute. Really. No more sofa sitting. No more underarms. No more silence.

130

"Did you say something?" asked Roddy Mix, and blinked.

"No," said Leslie, grinning her teeth out. Silence.

At nine-thirty Roddy Mix stood up, stretched, and said he ought to be going. Leslie stood at the same time, and looked sorry to see him go. At the doorway, Roddy looked as though he had something quite important to say, and looked hard at Leslie. False alarm. He leaned over and kissed the air around her face. "Night, Les," he said, taking the porch steps in one.

"Good night, Roddy," she answered. She stood on the porch until she couldn't see his taillights, and then walked inside humming.

12

Happy happy, thought Star. She pushed her legs busily through two feet of snow that lay in the park, and breathed lightly. The swings hung motionless, holding their breath in the frozen air. The slide was a slab of ice, untouched by any child since late November. Motionless.

Empty.

Star felt deliriously happy. She ran through the snow, and yanked at the swings. The frozen chains squawked in protest, but clanged like summer. Star leaped frantically onto the seesaw and banged it up and down—*crash, THUMP, crash, THUMP!*

Empty.

"Happy!" she cried, and smashed ice on the slide. "Well then, stupid girl," and clattered to the top of the monkey bars, "you're utterly—" and slid down the middle pole, stinging her legs through heavy woollen pants. She hit the ground with a shattering bang. "—unstable."

Empty!

Star looked around, satisfied, at the clanging park, shrieking gently in the frozen January air. She breathed heavily. Then she turned and headed for home.

13

"I hate her," Justina said flatly.

"Oh really!" But Leslie couldn't think of anything else to say and sat bleakly under Peter Frampton's 23″ x 35″ grin. She had been about to accuse Justina of being hopelessly dramatic again, but it occurred to her that Justina was not being dramatic. Justina hated Star, hated her as much as she had ever liked her. Well, thought Leslie, and well once more.

"I can't help it," Justina said, "I just do."

There was a silence, during which Leslie nodded sagely to her feet, and Justina drew hydronium atoms in her Chemistry book.

"Don't you?" she asked Leslie presently. "I mean, don't you just—hate her?"

"Well, HATE," said Leslie. "I don't think I could actually HATE anybody. I mean—hate. I don't know—afraid, maybe. Yeah—maybe."

Flash, thought Justina to herself.

"Actually," Leslie added, "I'm not sure about that. I'm just not sure."

On the wall, Peter grinned relentlessly, and on the floor Leslie sat and shivered.

14

The next Thursday, Star again thought she saw Nicky in the public library, but he had disguised himself in imitation fur and stacked heels, so she wasn't quite sure.

It didn't matter anyway.

15

In early February, Justina and Leslie sat uneasily in the Counselor's office and filled out their senior class schedules.

"I need—let's see here—three more credits," Justina announced. Her paper was heavy with black scribbles and crosses. Justina changed her mind frequently.

"Well," said Leslie, who didn't, "don't take Family Living, is all I can say."

"Oh Les," cried Justina, flinging her pencil to the floor, "isn't this *odd?* Just think. One more year, and we'll be out on our own. Lord. I don't know if I can handle that."

"Why are you always throwing things, Just?" Leslie delicately chewed the end of her eraser. Justina grimaced.

"Would you mind not gnawing on that? Gross."

"Mmmm. Have you taken Trig yet?"

"Lord no," Justina said, retrieving her pencil and stopping at the window on the way back. "There goes Star, heading for Mars. Lord."

"Why not?"

"Because I barely passed Geometry," said Justina, and sat heavily in her molded plastic chair. There were some rumpled napkins and a Mr. Coffee on the table. Justina picked up a fluted coffee filter and unfluted it.

"Justina!" said Leslie, scandalized, and looking around uneasily. "Put that down, for heaven's sake! Honestly."

"But think, really," said Justina, tossing her head back. "Just think of it, Les. In about—let's see—sixteen months, we'll be in the outside world. God."

"No," Leslie said practically. She made a careful X in the Advanced Algebra/Trigonometry box. "Most likely, I will be at the U. I'll possibly go to school the rest of my life. People do, you know."

"Oh Les, why do I put up with you?" Justina said. She pushed a rope of hair aggressively out of her eyes, and let her mouth hang open.

"You thirsty, Just?" Leslie looked. "Come on, here. Would you finish your schedule? I want to leave." She drummed her pencil lightly on the table.

Justina snapped her mouth shut. She picked up her own pencil, took a deep breath, and heavily marked a straight row of X's on her paper. "There now," she said. "Listen. Comparative Cultures. Government. Contemporary Novels. Family Living."

"Oh Justina, I don't think—"

"Family Living. Advanced Science. Mass Media."

They handed in their schedules, and headed for home. Wind battered at their ears, and no one talked much.

"Oh but Justina," Leslie wailed as they parted at the corner. "Family *Living*. Really."

16

Happy happy, thought Star, walking to school alone. Across the street, a slushy February wind fluffed the steam-curled hair of Justina and Leslie. Star looked nostalgically at their corduroy-entombed thighs, and hated the both of them. She pressed her face to the sky, and felt her feet push ahead on their own. Fourteen blocks. Fourteen.

"Shelter," she said out loud, reflectingly, *"shelter . . ."*

At school she pushed her jacket and scarves into her locker, and removed a notebook. She felt oddly detached from her surroundings. Vaseline on her lips. Down to the library for first-hour study hall. She met Justina on the way down, flying past, and said nothing. "Although," she told herself, settling into an armchair, "I probably should have. Said something."

The armchairs were hollowed by thousands of first-hour study bodies, and Star shifted for some time before she was comfortable. Then it was an annoyed "Dammit," as she remembered to find herself something to read. Back to her seat with the newest *Soviet Life.*

She dreamed about a gold-haired boy with lashes fram-

ing water-colored eyes. And so she wasn't terribly surprised when a gentle shake on her shoulder brought
her eye to eye with Roddy Mix. "Well hello," she said,
barely blinking.

"Mind if I sit down here?" he said, sitting next to
her. Star noted that there seemed to be a spot of some
sort on his knee. Possibly mustard.

"Look," said Roddy Mix, folding his arms across his
chest. Macho. He frowned slightly. "I've got to ask you
something."

It could of course be paint, thought Star, and wondered if Roddy Mix was in any art classes. No. He wasn't
the type. Probably mustard. Star smiled.

"I want you to go to the Leap Year Dance with me,"
said Roddy Mix very fast.

"You've got mustard on your knee," Star said.

There was a silence. "It's paint," said Roddy Mix presently. He's clearing his throat, thought Star. "Everyone's
going, you know. Even Justina, although I have the terri-
ble feeling that she's expecting me to ask her." He
laughed. Short, dry, and anxious. He cleared his throat.

Star looked at the speckled ceiling. Oh help, she
thought, and I'd rather die. She smiled encouragingly
at Roddy Mix. Horrors, she thought, all dreadful girls
in blue polyester-rayon with lip gloss under their noses,
and chewing Double Bubble. Oh, and stiff little men
in leisure suits, and football belt buckles. I'll die. And
wet hands, and forced smiles, and apple-green hips, and
tinny music—

"Yes," she said, looking directly at Roddy Mix with a grim smile. "Yes, Ronnie, I'd love to go with you."

Unstable.

"Roddy," said Roddy Mix, and blinked.

17

"Well," said Justina Milford, a week before the Leap Year Dance. "Well at least we'll neither of us need a new dress, that's for sure." She barked a short humorless laugh. Snow trickled uneasily from the sky.

Leslie pulled her pixie hood around her and coughed. "It's a good thing," she said, "that I'm not going. Listen to this cough—I'm coming down with something."

"Asian flu is going around," Justina said gloomily. "Most likely we'll both get it." She picked up a handful of snow and coughed experimentally into her mitten. "Well. The whole thing is silly. What's he trying to prove, taking sappy Star to the dance?"

"Justina," said Leslie, squinting at Justina's stony profile, "why are you so upset? It's not as though Roddy Mix had been going with you, after all."

"Well," said Justina, hurling awkwardly at a stop sign. "You never know. Besides, I did think someone would ask me. You know, someone. But no"—*splat*, as the snow hit a parked car instead—"no one does. So we'll just sit and play canasta all night long." She reached down for more snow. "Which actually doesn't bother me, you know. High school activities are such a bore. It'll be nice to just relax, for once."

"For sure," said Leslie, muffled inside her hood. She knew very well that if Roddy Mix should happen to make it known that it was all a mistake, that he wasn't *really* taking sappy Star to the Dance, she would be only too glad to let Justina play canasta one-handed all night long. Her experiences with "Let's just sit and relax for once" weren't anything she'd care to repeat too often.

Leslie looked at Justina guiltily. "For sure," she repeated, trying to sound emphatic. "What are friends for?" The question hung in the air and then vanished.

"Well," said Justina, taking aim again. She tossed sidearm. Another parked car. She sighed. "She'll probably show up in burlap or something. You know. Then he'll be sorry."

"I hope so," Leslie said, doubtfully. "And then he can come back to me."

"Mmm," said Justina, doubting it. They were in front of Justina's house. No one had shoveled the sidewalks lately, and hard gray paths wound icily to the porch and skirted across the yard. Justina stamped her crepe soles. Chips flew.

"Lori is going with Derek," Leslie remarked idly. "Remember Derek?"

"Lord," said Justina flatly. "Well, she can have him." She waved and clattered to her front steps. The door

139

slammed. Leslie walked on. Across the street, one light blazed softly in a dark house. As Leslie watched, the light flickered and went out. The curtains were drawn together noiselessly.

"Lord," said Leslie, and bounced up the steps to her own warm house.

18

"You look very nice," said Star's mother. She stood back and squinted. Two faces in Star's mirror.

"I look like you," Star said in some surprise. A pause. "I don't think I like it."

"Well, thanks." Her mother laughed, and reached for Star's head. They'd been doing this for hours, this going on with hair and clothes and trips to the mirror. Star was nervous, her eyes were too bright, and she knew that her magazine faces were smirking from the walls.

"—for a long time," her mother was saying with ribbon in her mouth. "Really. At your age I'd been to more dances than I could count. There. Now, how do you feel, Star?"

It was odd, she thought, these faces in the mirror. She didn't feel like herself anymore, she didn't recognize these great bright eyes staring back at her. They belonged to someone else, and so did the long white dress made of something gauzy, and the thin gold chain at her throat, and the red ribbon tying her hair off her face. Someone else. Her mother, for instance, standing damp-eyed next to her, looking. That look! She didn't see Star either, she saw a strange person they'd made together from ribbon and gauze. Except that she liked that person, she wished that person lived with her all the time. And Star couldn't bear to look, she turned away.

"—leave you alone for a bit," her mother was going on happily. "I'll call you as soon as he gets here. Now. What did I do with those safety pins?"

Alone, she left the mirror gladly, and switched on her radio. *Shelter, shelter.* "Composure," she said out loud, liking the sound. "Composure." Ridiculous. Don't think. She was doing the right thing, yes, this was all necessary. Yes. Look how happy her mother was! She would be at the kitchen table now, not a thought, no more worries of a troubled daughter. Yes. Better all around. Star sighed and ran a finger along the teeth of her comb. But then, why— No. Not to think.

"Darling, he's here," her mother called up the stairs. It was her University voice. Again, the lost feeling came over Star, the odd feeling of being forced to be someone else. But he was here, here, waiting for this girl in ribbon and gauze. So. Yes. Here we go.

Down the stairs. She saw Roddy Mix below her, stiff in a dark suit, hair blazing under the hall light. He was wiping his hand on the back of his leg, look at that.

141

He must be nervous. Not her mother, though, not to-night.

"—small business in the city," Roddy Mix was saying. "Accountants and so on."

"How nice," her mother said. "How very nice." And seeing Star on the stairs, poised for flight, "Well, there you are. Everyone ready, now? I'm sure you'll have a lovely time."

At the door now. "Good-bye," said Star's mother. "Good-bye," Star said.

"Good-bye," said Roddy Mix, and blinked.

Dark in the car, dark and cool, with the dashboard lights shining dimly. Roddy Mix turned left and right, fourteen blocks up to the school. Through the window, Star could see other couples heading for the hill, mostly in '74 Mustangs and leisure suits. She closed her eyes. Necessary. Roddy Mix leaned over and turned the radio on.

"—*get some shelter,*" purred Mick Jagger, "*or ah'm gonna fade away—*"

Star's eyes flew open. Roddy Mix whistled aimlessly. A car shot by in the darkness and honked. "That'll be Derek," Roddy said unnecessarily. He started whistling "Stairway to Heaven"—da da da da da DA da—and put his hands at twelve o'clock on the steering wheel. Star felt gauze sticking to her thighs.

"You know," he said presently, in the manner of one making small talk, "I thought you were going to say no when I asked you to this thing." Star said nothing, she looked hard at the generator light. "In fact, I was sure you'd say no."

"Love! Sister, it's just a kiss away. . . ." Star hummed along.

"Probably," Roddy said, "you should've."

"Kiss away, kiss away," Star sang. Not to listen, not to think.

Parking lot now. Roddy Mix switched the radio off, and leaned on the steering wheel. "Listen to me," he said. "Star!"

"Hmm?" How funny, there was a tiny dot of sweat at the corner of his mouth. Look at that.

"Why didn't you say no?"

She could see that he wanted an answer. He was sitting very close to her, too close, she slid back until she felt the door handle in her back. Composure, she thought. "Because," she said, "because I have to do this. Because if I don't, I'm—I mean, I'm not right." She trailed off, and shrugged. "Doesn't matter. Necessary."

"Necessary? What's necessary?"

She waved a hand impatiently. "Oh! All this. This dressing up—look at me!—this being normal. This being right." She made a face. "Normal! God. I never thought I'd be saying this to you. To anyone, actually."

"Star," said Roddy Mix, "I can take you back. Back there, now. Do you want that?"

Did she want that? She couldn't think, not now, not in ribbon and gauze. Behind Roddy's shoulder, she could see the school building looming, stern and gray, dotted with light. From open doors she could hear music, a slow constant humming. Composure. But what did she want? She could feel his face in the darkness, watching her, she couldn't put him off this time. Think? No. Alec wouldn't, none of them would. Just girls like her, in ribbon and gauze, who looked in their mirrors and didn't recognize the faces they found.

"Star," said Roddy Mix. Something in his voice she didn't recognize. She looked up abruptly, he was starting the car. "You don't have to talk, Star. I'll take you back."

The relief she felt astonished her. It came in great waves, leaving her weak, so she leaned back and closed her eyes. Necessary! It wasn't necessary after all, none of this was, she should've known. Happy now. She watched the freeway in front of her, the thin black ribbon taking her back. She watched the other cars too, and the staggering fences along the side of the road, but she didn't once watch Roddy Mix, not once. And he said nothing.

Downtown was damp and foggy, and Star's gauze was clammy next to her skin. Two blocks down and one over. In the alley she got out of the car, calmly, as if underwater, and went slowly up the wooden steps as if in a dream. Flowerpots stood breathlessly around the edge of the stoop. She tapped the door gently, with a knuckle, and heard behind her a car door slam. And gravel crunching coldly. Roddy Mix, she supposed, but let him come, too late now. And after all, he had brought her back—oh god, the door swung open, and Connie's head poked cautiously out.

"Yes," she said, and her face swelled into a smile. Star had never seen her smile quite like that before, it was frightening. But not to think, don't think, she thought, no time—no— She stepped into the warm room, tripping a bit over gauze, and stood in silence.

"Well," she said, breathing hard and feeling blasts of February from the open door. "Here I am. I'm back. You've won, you know."

"Oh really, baby," came Meggie's voice from the shadows. "Don't be that way, now. Yes, you're back. But then, we all knew you would be, didn't we?"

"Of course." Connie beamed. She stood heavily maternal at Star's shoulder.

"We all knew," said Nicky, all teeth. "You didn't think you could get away from us, did you, then?"

Happy happy— There was champagne suddenly, quite a lot of it, slopping all around among the smiles. Holding her goblet in a newly sweatless hand, and feeling her gauze finally unsticking, Star remembered Roddy Mix. Roddy? She frowned. He had followed, she knew, he had stood close while she knocked at the door, she could still feel his breath on her ear. Roddy Mix. If only— No. She turned reluctantly, yes, there was a golden head by the doorway. And the lashes. Well then. "I just want to say," she started, breathing in. And then wondered what she could possibly say to him. Too late now, she sighed and looked hard at him.

It was Alec. Alec? Yes, the gold head was his, don't THINK. Happy happy. "What did you want to say?" he asked. Star shook her head. "Say it," he said softly. "Say it, Star."

"Oh do," Meggie said, her face careful and watching.

"Please," Nicky added benignly.

Star closed her eyes. I am insane, she thought, and smiled brightly. "I just want to say," she said quietly, "that I won't ever leave again. I won't. Because I—"

"Yes?" Meggie purred.

"Can't."

19

On the steps outside, Roddy Mix shut the door carefully behind him. He pulled the dark collar of his suit up around his ears. Damp. Damp and foggy.

He thought of Star, standing in the middle of the room in her ribbons and gauze, quite alone. His hand shot out toward the doorknob—surely he couldn't leave her here, surely he couldn't—

On the steps he stood, the wind in his hair, his hand uncertain on the doorknob. He felt helpless, he felt like stamping his feet in a rage for the things he was powerless to change. What! What could he do! If only she would talk to him, if only she would look at him and listen and let him take her hand—

Then he relaxed, his hand fell to his side. Nothing. There was nothing he could do. She would choose; she had chosen.

It was cold on the steps, standing in the wind. Gravel crunching underfoot, Roddy Mix sprinted resolutely for his car.

20

Spring arrived with Monday morning. Justina Milford and Leslie Armbruster wore pastels and walked slowly to school. Fourteen blocks.

"Lori says she didn't see Roddy Mix at the Dance," remarked Justina. The wind blew up from the south, great puffs that turned slush to air. Justina kicked listlessly at the sidewalk. "Didn't see Star either."

"Well," said Leslie with one hand down the back of her pants, "I'm—darn this—"

"What are you doing?"

"This blouse—polyester—won't stay— It won't stay tucked, you know." Leslie struggled silently, biting her lip. "Oh! I hate this."

"Personally," said Justina, "I'm sorry we ever got involved with her. And I wouldn't be surprised if she'd been on welfare or something. Really."

"I suppose . . ." said Leslie. They stopped at Vine

for the light, as they had done every day for five years. Five years of fourteen daily blocks. Leslie squinted into the sky. "But I did like her, you know," she added softly.

"Oh Les." Justina wrinkled her nose. "She was spacy. Spooky. Unstable. A real loser." She shrugged. Spring was here. "Forget her," she advised Leslie. "It's all over now."

"Oh Just," Leslie said. "I don't forget as easily as you do. I probably won't ever forget." But even as she spoke, Leslie spotted a familiar gold head coming off a school bus, and all thoughts of winter fled.

"Roddy Mix," she said. "I wonder . . ."

"Lord," said Justina, but she was smiling. Spring was here, and things were back to normal in her world.

ABOUT THE AUTHOR

Jina Delton was the same age as Star when she wrote TWO BLOCKS DOWN, her first published novel; and her realistic portraits of high school students prove she is a keen observer of her contemporaries. Born in St. Paul, Minnesota, she lived in Tomah and Hudson, Wisconsin, before returning to St. Paul, where she and her family now live. She is presently working part-time in a reference library while writing her fourth novel.